THE ENDURANCE OF WILDFLOWERS

THE ENDURANCE OF WILDFLOWERS

MICALEA SMELTZER

Page & Vine
An Imprint of Meredith Wild LLC

Cover Design by Emily Wittig Designs

Paperback ISBN: 979-8-9877583-1-1

For everyone who wanted a "little" bit more.

CHAPTER ONE

Halloween

"Trick-or-treat!" The kids chime in unison the moment the door opens.

"Aw, how cute! A little Tinkerbell and ... well, what are you?" The lady's question is to Seda, but I can tell she's shutting down since this is about the fourth or fifth person to ask.

How do none of these people recognize her?

"She's Dani," I explain. "From *Hocus Pocus*. She wanted to match me." I point to my own outfit I'm decked out in to become Sarah Sanderson while Thayer is dressed as Billy.

"Oh." The woman smiles, but it doesn't quite reach her eyes. "I see it now."

Does she?

Doubtful.

Next Halloween I'm bulk buying the DVD and reverse trick-or-treating by giving it to ignorant people who haven't watched the best Halloween movie to ever exist.

She puts some candy in each of their pumpkin-shaped buckets. The girls decorated them earlier in the week with glitter glue and stickers. It was a messy project, but their laughter and smiles have been worth the headache of finding glitter all over the house ever since. Not to mention the glue I had to pick off the table.

The door shuts, and we start back down the walkway to

where Thayer waits with the wagon. Caleb was supposed to be with us but ended up having to work late. I've sent him a million and one pictures to make up for it. Despite his immense workload, Caleb is a very present father, so when he misses out on the things he wants to be there for, I know it tears him up inside a little bit.

"Dad," Seda groans, swinging her bucket back and forth. "That woman didn't know who I was either. Are people stupid?" Her cheeks puff out with indignation.

"Seda," I scold, trying not to laugh since she caught me off guard with her statement. Kids really do say the darndest things. "Don't say things like that."

She rolls her eyes. "It's only the truth, Mom."

Somehow, she's already eight-years-old going on thirty. I don't know what I'm going to do when she's a teenager. Honestly, Thayer and Caleb are the ones I'm really worried about when she starts dating. There is no doubt in my mind that Caleb will be running background checks.

Soleil reaches out for her daddy, and he takes her from my arms. She's already two and I'd be lying if I didn't say I haven't cried about that fact at least once a week for the past month, especially with both girls fast approaching nine and three.

I always thought people were crazy when they said life passes in the blink of an eye, but they weren't lying.

I think it's made harder by the people I wish were here to see them.

My mom.

Forrest.

Sometimes it's hard not to look at Seda and think to myself that Forrest never got to do certain things. Life is a beautiful thing, but infinitely unfair.

"Do you want to stop at any more houses?" Thayer asks Seda, grabbing ahold of the handle on the wagon to pull it, despite my attempt to get it.

She shakes her bucket, stifling a yawn. "I'll never say no to more candy."

Thayer chuckles, his eyes sparkling in the glow from the streetlight when he smiles at me.

How is it that after all these years he still manages to take my breath away? I swear he only gets more handsome as time passes. Happiness looks good on my husband.

"All right," he says to Seda as we continue down the street. "We'll stop at two more houses and go home. Ms. Tink here is snoring on my shoulder. I think there might be drool too."

Seda laughs, skipping ahead of us. "Is she really?" Soleil gives out a snore just then that's loud enough to wake the dead. "Maybe we should just do one more?" she suggests.

"If you're okay with that." I set Soleil's bucket in the wagon. "Let me take that," I tell Thayer, pointing to the wagon handle.

"Nah, I've got it," he insists. Stubborn man.

Seda runs up to the next house and once she has her candy we head back home. Luckily, it's only a three-minute walk to get there. I'm sure Binx and Winnie will be more than happy to have us back.

"Is Daddy home yet?" Seda asks us, eyeing Caleb's house next-door.

It's funny how it no longer feels like my mom's house. Caleb has fixed it up over the past few years, some small projects here and there, but it's all added up to make it look like a whole new place.

"I don't know." The house is dark, but that doesn't mean much. "Let's go see."

"I'll put Soleil to bed." Thayer leans over and gives me a kiss.

"Thank you." He heads up the driveway, towing the wagon, while I walk over to Caleb's with Seda.

She runs up to the front door, candy bucket clasped in her hands and rings the doorbell.

I stand back a few feet, waiting to see if he comes to the door. He didn't reply to my last text message, but that doesn't mean much. If he made it in, then he probably wanted to eat and shower.

Seda frowns when the door doesn't open. "I guess he's not home."

"Ring it again just in case."

She bites her lip and pushes the button.

This time, the front porch light flicks on and her whole face lights up. I'll forever be thankful that she has the bond that she does with Caleb. Since he isn't her biological father, he could've easily turned his back on her after our divorce, but he never did. That's just not Caleb. She's not his daughter by blood, but in all the ways that count they're father and daughter.

He opens the door, his hair damp from the shower and holds back his overactive golden retriever puppy he's only had for a few weeks.

"Trick-or-treat, Daddy!" Seda holds out her bucket eagerly.

He chuckles, opening the door. "I've got your favorite. Hold on."

"Mommy?" Seda looks at me over her shoulder, blonde hair swinging with the movement. She looks so much like me at that age that it's like seeing a version of who I could've been as a child if I hadn't had my father. "Is it okay if I stay the night at Daddy's?"

Caleb arches a brow, waiting for my response. "I don't mind."

"It's okay with me."

"Yay!" She hugs Caleb, dashing inside while the puppy follows her.

"She's hyper tonight, and she hasn't even had her candy yet," I warn him.

He smiles. "I can handle it."

I know he can.

I wave before crossing the lawn to my house with Thayer. Inside, I find him in Soleil's room, tucking her into bed. She's awake now, but her eyes are heavy.

"Hi," I mouth from the doorway.

He motions for me to come into the room, and I join him beside her bed, the two of us taking turns reading the story. She's exhausted from her night of trick-or-treating and falls asleep before we make it to the last page. I tuck the blankets around her and kiss the top of her head.

I love being a mom. It's hard, that's for sure, and certainly not for everyone but I love my children more than anything in the world. I think I was always meant to be a mom. Thayer and I have been trying for another, but getting pregnant hasn't been easy this time around. We agreed we'd love to have one more, but perhaps that isn't in the cards for us. I guess, only time will tell.

Thayer takes my hand, leading me to our room. "Seda's staying with Caleb?"

Heat infuses his eyes, and I know what he's thinking. "Yes." My voice sounds breathy, and he grins. Damn him. It's not my fault I have the hots for my husband. With two young kids it can be hard to fit in time for just the two of us. We try to have a date night at least once a month, to go out and be able to talk without hearing "Mommy" and "Daddy" repeated fifty times in a row.

"So, it's just you ... me ... and a passed-out toddler?"

"And Binx and Winnie," I remind him. "Can't forget the animals."

He chuckles, lowering his head to press his lips to the curve of my neck. "I really like this costume." He grabs my waist, pulling me against him. It's impossible not to feel the hard curve of his erection. "I've been thinking about taking it off of you for a ridiculous amount of time." He eyes my breasts where they're pushed up, nearly spilling out of the top thanks to my tightly laced corset.

I gasp, grasping his forearms when he trails wet kisses down my neck. That spot is so sensitive on me, and he gets great pleasure from kissing me there. I think he likes knowing he can still make me weak in the knees.

"I need to shower," I giggle from the sensation of his beard tickling my skin.

"I can shower with you. If you want?" He pulls away, hands on my cheeks.

I stand on my tiptoes to kiss him, more than a little eager to get my husband naked. "Yes."

We undress each other on our way into the bathroom. It takes a ridiculous amount of time to undo my corset, but eventually he manages.

He reaches in to turn the shower on, then immediately drops to his knees in front of me, forcing my legs open.

"Thayer," I gasp, my fingers sinking into his hair as his tongue works against me. I hadn't been expecting that at all—not that I'm going to complain. My head falls back against the wall. I moan when his fingers join his mouth. It's been years now, and the sex between us has never gotten stale. If anything, it's gotten better. The familiarity makes it easy to ask for what you want, what you need. "More," I beg, tugging on his hair.

I feel his chuckle vibrate against me. It sends a shiver up my spine.

I mewl in protest when he stops, looking up at me from his knelt position on the floor, slowly stroking his cock. I bite my lip at the sight. "You wanna come on my tongue, Sunshine?" I nod breathlessly, biting my lip to hold in a whimper. "Say it, baby. I need to hear you say it."

"I ... wanna ... come ... on ... your mouth."

He doesn't say anything. Grabbing the back of my thighs in his strong hands he holds me still, working his tongue against my clit.

"Yes, yes, yes," I chant, my body growing boneless. Thayer knows my body better than I do at this point and works me just the right way. "Right there. Don't stop."

He chuckles, probably at my breathless tone.

When my orgasm shatters through me, he's there to catch me, scooping me into his arms and carrying me into the shower where he scrubs me clean, paying extra attention to certain areas.

He doesn't fuck me in the shower, but he does get me desperate and aching for more, downright begging by the time he drags me from the shower to dry me with a towel.

"You're being mean," I tell him, only half-serious.

He grins up at me, finishing drying my legs. "You like it," is all he says before he picks me up and carries me out of the bathroom, only to toss me down on the bed and cover my body with his.

He's big and strong, his body swallowing mine beneath him.

Brushing his nose over mine, he then kisses me.

Slow. Sensual. Making me ache even more. He grips my hips, holding me still when I try to grind against him.

He chuckles, nipping at my chin playfully. "You're always so eager."

I whimper as his mouth moves down my body, swirling his tongue around my right nipple and then the left. Reaching down, I go to wrap my hand around his erection, but he twines his fingers with mine, pinning my hand and then the other, above my head.

"Thayer." I try to escape his hold, but it's futile.

"Let me have my fun." He kisses the curve of my neck.

"What about my fun?" I pout, jutting out my bottom lip.

He pulls away slightly so he can grin down at me. "That's what round two is for."

Thayer takes his time teasing me, so that when he finally pushes inside me my body is more than ready to welcome him.

Sometimes I wonder how it can continue to be this good, this intense every single time. Our chemistry both in the bedroom and outside of it, is unparalleled. I was so young when I first fell for Thayer, I really didn't have a full grasp on love or even life yet, but what I feel for him has endured through numerous trials and tribulations.

"God, you feel so good, baby," he rasps in my ear. "You have no idea how good this sweet pussy feels wrapped around my cock."

I claw at his back, silently begging for more.

Harder.

Faster.

Everything he has to give me.

His fingers find my clit, rubbing with just the right pressure and intensity.

"Yes, oh God yes, right there." I cry out, grabbing onto his biceps when my orgasm shatters through me.

"Oh, fuck. Baby, I—" He grips my hips tighter, holding me in place through his own orgasm.

Spent, he rolls over and tugs me along with him so that I'm lying practically halfway across his body.

Brushing his lips over my forehead, he whispers, "I think I did it that time."

I stifle a yawn. "Did what?"

"Got you pregnant," he answers in a tone like I should know already what he meant. I suppose I should have, but I'm blaming the two incredible orgasms he gave me, plus being tired, on the fact that my brain isn't fully functioning at the moment.

"Hmm, maybe." Forcing my eyes open, I stare at the side of his face. The slope of his nose and curve of his lips. Thayer Holmes is one hot specimen of man and he's all mine.

"What would you do ... How would you feel if I don't get pregnant again?"

He gives me a funny look. "You will."

"But what if I don't?" I give voice to the fear that's been niggling in the back of my mind.

I'm incredibly blessed to have two smart, amazing little girls. Perhaps that's all the universe thinks I'm meant to have. I'd be okay with that, but would he? Especially after having lost one child?

The hole of Forrest's life is felt every day. That's not something that goes away, not even for me who wasn't even his parent. I know another child wouldn't replace him. That's not what I'm meaning at all. Just that maybe, after such a devastating loss, he wants a bigger family than I might be capable of giving him.

"Where's this coming from?"

I sigh, tucking my hair behind my ear. I'm totally ruining the post coital bliss, but this is a conversation I need to have.

"I don't know ..." I hedge, searching for the right words. "With Seda and Soleil it happened pretty easily and quickly." I blush, thinking about how Seda was a total surprise. "That hasn't been the case this time. And I'm okay with that, if all we have is our two girls, but are you all right with that?"

He stares at me for a moment, processing what I've said. "Fuck, Salem, of course I am."

"Good. That's good." I start to tear up, annoyed at myself for feeling emotional about this. "I want another baby, too, but ..." I trail off, not even sure of what I want to say, let alone how to process my thoughts.

Many women struggle with fertility and I'm so lucky to have my two little girls, but my heart yearns for at least one more. I love being a mom. It's the hardest job out there, but my daughters are truly the best things I've ever done in this world. I would love to bring another child into this world. Another girl or a boy, it's doesn't matter. I just know there's room in my heart for more kids to love.

"Salem." He says my name softly, reverently, tucking my naked body impossibly closer to his. My body melts against him. Thayer Holmes is my happy place. "Whatever is meant to be is what will be."

I give a small giggle. "You sound like a magic eight ball."

He pinches my side playfully. "Don't laugh at me."

I trace my finger around his nipple. "I just don't want to disappoint you."

He shifts suddenly so I'm beneath him and he's holding his weight above me. "I can't believe you'd ever think that. You're the love of my life. You could never disappoint me, and definitely not over something like this."

I wrap my arms around his neck. "I'm overthinking this, aren't I?"

"You are." He kisses my forehead. "I don't want you feeling stressed—not about having another baby. Do you want to stop trying?"

I shake my head. "No."

"Do you want me to see a doctor?"

It surprises me he would offer, but then again maybe I shouldn't be so shocked. This is Thayer after all.

"I don't know. Maybe we both should?"

He nods. "I'll schedule an appointment."

"Thank you." I tilt my head up to kiss him. "Did I ruin the mood for round two?"

He grins, shaking his head. "Definitely not."

CHAPTER TWO

A week and a half later

Sunshine Cupcakes might be my place of business, but it's also my special place—the one where I feel closest to my mom. Checking the time, I silently curse to myself and dust my hands off. Powdered sugar goes flying everywhere. Not a day goes by that I don't go home covered in the stuff.

"What is it?" Susanne asks, looking up from the cupcake she's frosting to look like a flower. I thought it would be a fun idea to sell cupcake bouquets, and they've become a hit in our small town. People order them for birthdays, weddings, and whatever else they want them for. We've even started doing seasonal ones, which is what Susanne is working on now.

"Student teacher meetings," I explain, pulling my apron over my head and hanging it on the hook. Washing my hands, I say, "I have to meet Thayer and Caleb there."

Luckily for me, the school isn't far from my shop. I didn't mean to let the time get away from me, but when I get in the zone with my baking, I tend to forget reality.

"Is everything okay?"

"Yeah, yeah." I smooth my hair down, checking my appearance in the camera of my phone. "It's just a normal meeting. Seda isn't in trouble or anything. I'll be back right after."

This time it's Susanne who looks at the clock. "You don't

need to come back. Take the rest of your day off with your sweet family. Hannah and I can hold down the fort here."

Susanne and Hannah are always encouraging me to let them handle things more. It's not that I'm a control freak—okay, maybe a little—but I truly love being at my little shop.

I frown, biting my lip. "Are you sure?"

"Absolutely." She shoos me to the back door.

"Well, if you're sure ... Just call me if I need to come back."

"We can handle it. Get to your meeting."

Shrugging my coat on, I grab up my purse and say goodbye before getting into my SUV. I haven't even backed out of the space when the console lights up with a phone call from Thayer.

"Hey," I answer, putting the vehicle in reverse. "Time got away from me. I'm on my way, though."

His chuckle echoes over the line. "I got a call from the preschool that Soleil was running a fever, so I just picked her up and I'm taking her to the pediatrician since they had an opening to squeeze her in. It'll just be you and Caleb for the meeting. I hope that's all right."

"Is she okay?" I ask, my motherly worry kicking in. I hate when one of the kids is sick. It's so helpless seeing one of my children hurting. Especially when they're as young as Soleil and can't always articulate what's bothering them. "Do I need to come with you? Caleb could handle it. I—"

"There's nothing more you can do for Soleil than I can. Besides, I'm almost to the doctor's office and it's on the other side of town. Go to the school, and I'll text you when I know something. Right now, she's fine."

"All right." I turn in the direction of the school. "Okay. Give her kisses from me, okay?"

"You know I will."

He ends the call just as I'm turning into the lot of the school. Caleb is already there, sitting inside his own vehicle. When he sees me, he climbs out and wait by his driver's side.

Hopping out, I grab my purse and slap a beanie down over my head to cover my ears from the cold. I can't imagine living anywhere else. I love Hawthorne Mills, but the frigid winters can be a bit much at times.

"It's just us," I tell Caleb as we head toward the school's entrance, "Soleil got sick at preschool, so Thayer is taking her to the doctor."

He frowns, scratching at the light blond stubble on his jaw. "I'm sorry. Is she okay?"

"He says she is. It's probably just a cold or something. I swear, this time of year all kids do is pass sickness back and forth. Sometimes I wonder if it's worth having her in preschool."

At the door, we have to show our IDs to the camera before we're buzzed in.

We head down the hall together towards Seda's classroom. "Let me know if you want Seda to stay with me while Soleil is sick. You know I don't mind."

"I know." I smile, squeezing his arm. "Seda can do whatever she wants."

She's at the age now where we kind of let her do her own thing, as far as where she wants to be and for the most part, she unintentionally splits the time equally. And since all of us get along and there's no animosity, we spend holidays and her birthday together.

Ms. Bloom's classroom has an explosion of paper flowers decorating the outside of her door and part of the wall space.

"Whoa," Caleb says, taking it all in. "This is cool."

"Isn't it?"

Inside the room, Ms. Bloom sits behind her desk. Much like the outside of her classroom, the inside is an explosion of colors. She's been a great teacher to Seda, probably the best she's had so far. She's young too, fresh out of college. It's her first year here.

She smiles when we enter the room. "Mrs. Holmes, it's so good to see you."

"Hi." I smile, sliding into one of the student's desks near hers. "How are you?"

"I'm good. And you are?" She holds a hand out to Caleb.

"Oh, um ... I'm Caleb." He clears his throat. "Caleb Monroe. Seda's dad?" It comes out as a question, and I can't help but snicker.

Caleb shoots me a look.

Ms. Bloom is certainly pretty, and I can't help but think Caleb might be a tad smitten. He hasn't had a chance to meet her yet this year, having missed back-to-school night in August because of work.

Ms. Bloom blushes, and now I'm really trying not to laugh. Apparently, the attraction isn't only one-sided.

"I didn't know that your husband wasn't Seda's father," she says, then immediately covers her mouth with her hand. "I'm so sorry. Please pretend I didn't say that. That was so unprofessional of me."

I laugh. "I'm not easily offended, and he is her father. It's kind of a complicated story, actually, but Caleb is my ex-husband, but he's raised Seda. Thayer and I got back together after my divorce with Caleb, but Caleb is still very much Seda's father, even if it's not by DNA."

"Wow." Her eyes flick between us. "That is ... quite the story." *And she doesn't even know the half of it.* "Well, it's nice to meet you, Caleb. I'm Ms. Bloom, Seda's third grade teacher."

"It's nice to meet you, too." Caleb tries to maneuver his body into one of the small kid's chairs but gives up and ends up standing.

Both of us watch him with amusement.

"Seda is such a joy to have in class. Truly. She's incredibly kind and caring. Smart, too. She never acts out in class and always does her work. But—" *Oh no.* "—she is having some trouble with reading, so that's the reason I wanted to meet today. I'm happy to stay after school with her a few times a week to work on it. It's not so bad that I think she needs outside intervention, just a little more one-on-one time. I think if we all work together, we could get her reading at her age level or above by the end of the school year."

"Oh, I ..." I hadn't noticed that she was having trouble and immediately feel like I've failed her in some way. "I didn't know."

Ms. Bloom gives me a reassuring smile. "Please, don't beat yourself up about it. It took me a while to catch on too. She's good at hiding it."

Caleb clears his throat. "It's kind of you to offer to stay later with her, but you have your own life. You don't need to stay at work longer than necessary."

She laughs. "Trust me, it's fine. What else am I going to do? Go home and knit?" She blushes yet again. "Not that knitting is bad, I actually enjoy it—but I ... I'm getting off topic, sorry." She shakes her head. "What I mean is, I have the free time and it's no trouble at all."

I bite my lip, exchanging a look with Caleb. "If you're positive you're okay with it."

"Absolutely. I was thinking we could do Monday, Wednesday, and Fridays if that's okay with everyone? I think an extra hour after school will do the trick."

"Okay." I nod. "We can make that work."

Between the three of us, there should always be someone who can pick her up.

She goes over a few more things before the meeting is over.

Caleb and I head out, but I don't miss the way he turns back to look at her before we're fully out of the classroom.

I wait until we're down the hall before I blurt out, "You like Seda's teacher!"

"No!" He says way too quickly. "I just met her right now. You know that."

"But you think she's pretty. You can't lie to me, Caleb. I know you."

He sighs, running his fingers through his golden blond hair. "She is pretty," he agrees, "but she's Seda's teacher."

I arch a brow. "So?"

"So?" He repeats, laughing. "Salem, I can't exactly ask out our daughter's teacher on a date. I'm pretty sure that's illegal."

I playfully slap his arm. "You're a lawyer. You know it isn't illegal. But if you like her, you should ask her out."

Caleb stops walking, grabbing my wrist so that I halt with him. "Why?"

I blink at him. "Huh?"

"Why do you want me to ask her out so bad?"

I look back down the hall, where the classroom sits on the end with an explosion of paper flowers. "I was getting the vibes she was into you, and you were into her, so I just thought—"

"And it has nothing at all to do with you feeling guilty that I'm still single?"

I lower my head. He has me there. Sure, Caleb has dated some since our divorce but nothing that was ever serious. I want him to find someone, not because of guilt or selfishness, but because Caleb is a genuinely great guy who deserves to find the love like I have with Thayer. I've always been sorry I couldn't be that for him, but I know when he finds his own person he'll understand.

"I don't feel guilty," I finally answer, forcing myself to look him in the eyes. "I just want you to be happy."

He arches a brow in challenge. "And I need a girlfriend to be happy?"

I start to wiggle. "Well, no—but you guys clearly had chemistry. If you want to go for it, then you should."

He sighs, letting my wrist go. "I'm too busy to date."

"Caleb," I say softly, hesitantly, "when we were married you were never too busy for me or Seda. You always made time for us despite your workload."

His eyes narrow. "What are you getting at?"

I shrug. "Just that we make time for the things, the people, we love. When," I emphasize, letting him know I'm not trying to pressure him, "you're ready to get back out there, you'll find the time."

We start toward the front of the school again, and he doesn't say anything until we reach the doors. "You're right. When it's right, there will be time."

I give him a soft smile. I just want him to be happy, whatever that is for him, and I know him well enough to know that he's not entirely there yet. "Do you want to come over for dinner tonight? I'm making taco salad."

He smiles, but there's still something in his eyes. He looks back at the school as we start through the lot, and I wonder if he's thinking about Ms. Bloom or if there's something more on his mind.

When we reach our cars, he finally speaks again. "I'll never say no to a dinner I don't have to make."

He flashes me a smile and slips into his car.

I do the same. I have a sick little girl to get home to.

CHAPTER THREE

Seda snuggles on the couch with a sick Soleil. I've long ago given up on trying to keep her away from her little sister when she's sick. Seda has a natural mothering streak, so anytime Soleil doesn't feel quite right she takes over trying to make her feel better. Tonight, after Caleb left, that meant she put on Soleil's favorite movie, and they've cuddled on the couch ever since.

"I'll finish up here and make hot chocolate for all of us." Thayer drops a kiss on the side of my forehead, swiping the disinfectant wipe from me in the process so I'll stop cleaning the counters.

When one of the kids is sick, I go into obsessive cleaning mode. I got especially paranoid after a stomach bug I caught from Seda last year. It was a brutal week here at the Holmes's when we all came down with it.

"Get off your feet and sit with the girls."

Sometimes I can't help but wonder if this man is real.

"I was almost done," I protest, trying to get the wipe back from him.

"And now you're fully done." He winks, swatting me on the ass. "I won't be long."

I know there's no point in arguing with him, so I join the girls in the family room where one of the Tinkerbell movies is playing. One day I put it on randomly in the hopes of keeping Soleil entertained while I cleaned the house and she's been hooked ever since.

She snuggles her older sister, her thumb stuck between her lips.

It's a habit I've tried so hard to break her of, but whenever she's overly tired or doesn't feel good somehow her thumb ends up in her mouth.

"Come here, Mom." Seda pats the empty spot beside her, lifting up the blanket she's under to make room for me.

I smile, joining them. Seda covers my legs with the blanket. I've barely sat down when Binx hops up, curling into the crook of my legs. Winnie is in the corner, shaking a stuffed lobster back and forth.

"Dad's making hot chocolate," I whisper to her, brushing my fingers through her hair with a gentle touch.

She gasps, eyes widening with excitement. Thayer's hot chocolate is a big deal around here. It really is the best, though.

"He is?"

I nod. "First hot chocolate of the season."

Soleil lets her thumb drop from her mouth. "Hot chocolate?"

I love the way she says chocolate right now. Toddlers have this unique way of making words their own and she slurs the letters together with a slight lisp while putting emphasis on the late part, but it sounds more like let.

"Yes, but only a little bit for you since you don't feel good." I reach across Seda's lap, tapping Soleil's nose when she frowns.

"I feel better. *Pwomise.*"

It's a few minutes before Thayer joins us with a tray of mugs and a snack of chocolate covered pretzels. The man knows how to spoils us, which is both a good and bad thing.

"Chocolate." Soleil makes grabby hands, beckoning him to hand her a mug.

He chuckles. "Hold on, little princess." He carefully passes out the cups.

Seda gasps, staring down into her mug. "Is that a marshmallow shaped like a snowman?"

He chuckles, relaxing into the couch. "It is."

"And peppermint chips?"

"You betcha." He settles on the couch beside Soleil, leaving the girls sandwiched between us.

I raise the cup to my lips, taking a sip. Outstanding. "You're too good for us."

He winks. "I can't help it."

Soleil sips at her much smaller cup. "Yummy. Ahh." She smacks her lips loudly.

She's taken to saying *ahh* after every sip of a drink ever since Thayer's brother, Laith, taught it to her when he visited over the summer.

"You wanted to watch Tinkerbell again?" Thayer ruffles her short blonde curls in jest.

She nods, holding her tiny mug in both hands, eyes glued to the TV.

Thayer looks at me, shaking his head with an amused smile. I'm pretty sure it's in the parenting handbook somewhere that you must get used to watching the same movie or show non-stop.

It isn't long before Thayer has to take the cup from Soleil as she falls over asleep, mouth hanging open and snoring way louder than most adults.

"I'll carry her up to bed," he mouths to me, maneuvering off the couch gently enough to not disturb her before scooping her into his arms. Thayer is a pro when it comes to picking up a sleeping child and keeping them asleep. Me? Not so much. So, I always leave that job for him.

"How about you? Are you ready for bed?" I nudge Seda slightly.

She spent the day off from school at her friend's house, and from what she said at dinner they had a busy day playing.

"Can I stay up just a little longer?"

Her eyes are heavy. I know she's sleepy, but I nod anyway when she snuggles closer to me. She's getting older and, with a toddler, sometimes it's tough to find moments of one-on-one time with her. I try and make an effort to do something once a month just the two of us. Thayer and Caleb try to do the same with her as well. She's handled everything over the past few years with such grace, adjusting fairly seamlessly to the situation with having two dads.

"Do you want me to put something else on?"

"What about one of those Hallmark movies? I love those."

She truly is my daughter. I scoop up the remote, switching off the movie. "Sure. Let's see what's on."

The movie has already been on for about forty minutes, but Seda doesn't seem to mind. She lays her head in my lap, getting comfy. I stroke my fingers through her soft blonde hair.

Looking down at her, I can't get over how grown up she's getting. I don't want to think about it too much, but the teen years are around the corner, and then before I know it, she'll be leaving for college or whatever it is she decides to do. She'll be making her own way in the world.

"Mom?"

My fingers still in her hair. "Yeah?"

"I can feel you staring at me."

I chuckle. "Sorry."

She rolls over so she's looking up at me. "Why were you

looking at me?"

I smile softly. "I was just thinking about how much I love you."

"Oh. Okay. I love you, too, Mom."

She turns back to face the TV and Thayer returns to join us on the couch.

My breath catches for a moment when I think about the fact that I'm sitting here with him, with our daughters, and I'm living the life I wasn't sure I would ever have. I wish some things had happened differently, and my heart yearns for my mom to still be here with us, and Forrest too, but I think all things considered, we're doing all right.

And sometimes, all right is more than enough.

CHAPTER FOUR

The door chimes at the entrance for Sunshine Cupcakes. I look up from the tray of cupcakes I'm carefully balancing to add to the case to find Thayer walking into the store. I bite my lip to hide my smile, because he has no right looking so good in a pair of jeans, a Carhartt jacket, and beanie pulled low over his ears.

"Hey," he smiles at me, eyes crinkling at the corners, "got any cookie dough cupcakes?"

My heart swells. "For you? Always."

Will there ever come a time when this man doesn't make me swoon?

No, I don't think so.

I slide the tray of hot fudge sundae cupcakes into the case and snag a cookie dough, handing it across the counter.

Thayer knows I won't take his money, so he tucks a ten-dollar bill into the tip jar. I don't complain since I let all the tips go to Hannah and Susanne.

He unwraps the cupcake, taking a bite. "How's your day been?"

"Busy." I look down at my dirty apron. I've been baking for hours and hours at this point. Some days are sluggish with customers, but today was not one of those days. "It's finally slowing down."

"Do you have time for lunch?" He must notice my look of doubt because he quickly adds, "I can pick something up and bring it back here."

I nod. "That should work."

"Cool, I'll be back." He leans over the counter to kiss me, before heading outside to his parked truck.

The swoosh of the swinging door that leads to the kitchen has me turning my head. Hannah gives a dreamy sigh, hand to her chest. "Not that I was eavesdropping or anything, but one day I want a man like Thayer."

I laugh lightly. "I hope you find him." I want to tell her that she's barely twenty and has plenty of time to find the one for her, but considering I fell for Thayer when I was eighteen, I don't have any room to judge. Love finds us at all different times of our lives. Sometimes, it's puppy love, or the kind of love that's there to teach you something, and if you're lucky you find that rare and perfect true love. I know that's the kind Thayer and I have, but it doesn't mean the road to happiness was easy. We spent years apart.

"I need you to take a look at these red velvet cupcakes. They didn't rise properly and I'm not sure if they're workable or I should throw them out."

"Let me see."

She pushes back into the kitchen with me following. The cupcakes sunk in the middle a significant amount. They're definitely not something I want to sell at full price.

"Go ahead and frost them and we'll use them as free samples until they run out."

She gives me a thumbs up. "Sounds like a plan."

Since Hannah and Susanne have the kitchen covered, I head back out front to tend to any customers who come in. I much prefer to be in the kitchen baking, but I make it a habit to rotate the jobs I handle in the store. Especially since I think it's good to form a relationship with my customers. Looking around the space, I can't help but smile to myself. It looks vastly different from when it was my mom's antique shop.

I've only recently started delving into candle making once more. Seda was curious about it when she learned it was something I used to do. I decided to get out my old supplies, order some new, and teach her. We've been making candle scents to match the cupcakes we sell and it's been a surprising hit. Sometimes, we'll do a one-off scent when Seda wants to try something, like bubblegum or Fruity Pebbles.

In the time it takes Thayer to return, there's another small surge of customers. He waits patiently at one of the tables with our food until it slows down enough for me to let Hannah handle it.

Hanging up my apron, I wash my hands and join him at the table.

He passes my food over to me. I didn't feel hungry until he slid it across the table and the scent of fries hits my nose. I pop a fry in my mouth, reaching for the drink. The Diet Coke is a much-needed pleasure to get me through the rest of the day.

"Are you done with work?" I ask him. Sure, it's early yet, but with winter approaching, it affects the amount of business he has until we start getting regular snow and he plows the lots he has contracts with.

He nods, unwrapping his burger. "It's been a slow day." Clearing his throat, he says, "I got a call back from the doctor's office."

"Oh?" I arch a brow. "On the um ..."

He chuckles when I blush. "On the sperm count thing? Yes. They can't get me in for a test until March."

My shoulders sag. I wasn't able to book with my gynecologist for a checkup until January, and that was pure luck since they'd just had a cancellation. Though, they did add me to the list if there were any other cancellations to bump me up. My doctor wouldn't give me a referral for a fertility specialist until he saw me again. Freaking doctors.

"Hey," he says softly, reaching across the table to gently urge my chin up with the tip of his finger. "We'll get answers. I promise. And who knows," he grins, letting his finger drop, "maybe it'll happen on its own."

I exhale heavily, giving him a small smile. "I wish I could have your optimism."

"Luckily for you, I have enough for the both of us."

That he does.

CHAPTER FIVE

"Look at me doing my Christmas shopping early. This has to be some kind of record or something." Georgia spins excitedly in front of me.

It's rare for us to have a whole day to spend together, but her husband Michael, Thayer, and Caleb are watching all the kids so we can hang out together.

We already got our nails done before coming to the mall to do some shopping for the holidays. As excited as she is to be starting her buying early, I decide not to tell her that I began over the summer—purchasing things here and there when they were on sale and forcing Thayer to stash them in the attic.

"I don't know where to even go first." Georgia twirls again, a mixture of excitement and awe. "I never get to go shopping without the kids anymore."

"I'm glad we could do this," I say, trying to steer her away from the aggressive kiosk man since she's not paying attention and he's about two seconds away from coating her hands in lotion or something. "It's so hard to get together the older we get."

"You're telling me." She darts away, her eyes getting big at a store full of women's clothing. "Oh, look at that scarf. It's beautiful." She shakes her head roughly. "I'm shopping for the kids. For the kids," she chants.

I laugh, grabbing her hand. "Come on, let's go this way. There's a LUSH around the corner and I want to grab some things for Seda."

"Ooh, that's a good idea. I might get some things too." I raise a brow at her, and she grins. "What? I have to help Michael with my stocking."

We reach the store, and she darts over to the section with perfumes and lotions while I make a beeline for the bath bombs. It doesn't take me long to pick a few I know Seda will like before I'm browsing the store to see if there's anything else she might like. In the background Christmas music plays, trying to get us all in the jolly spirit.

I bump into Georgia who tries to hide her basket behind herself. With a sigh, she realizes there's no hiding it. "I told you, Michael needs help," she says, defensively.

I don't know if it's that the poor guy needs that much help or Georgia is just particular about gifts. For years, she'd put together a thorough Christmas list for our mom, even sorting them into categories.

"You don't have to defend yourself to me." I bump her hip playfully as I walk by.

About fifteen minutes later we're leaving the store weighed down with bags, and I can't even judge Georgia because I ended up snagging a few things for myself too.

"Where to next?"

"Mmm." She thinks. "I need to run into the video game store for the boys and Michael. And Victoria needs some new shoes. There's a doll I want to get her too," she muses, trailing off.

"Should we divide and conquer? Then meet up for lunch."

She worries her lip between her teeth. "Are you sure? We're supposed to be catching up. God knows when we'll have this opportunity again?"

"We caught up some at the nail salon and we'll continue over lunch."

"This is true. Meet in the food court in two hours?"

"Sounds perfect."

She heads in one direction, and I go in the other.

Two hours feels like plenty of time, but when I check my phone and see I need to meet up with Georgia in just ten minutes, I decide that it's actually no time at all. But I did manage to get some things for Thayer and the girls too. I won't have much more left to get that hopefully I'll be able to snag online.

Juggling my bags, I book it to the nearest elevator and take it to the top floor where the food court is.

I burst into laughter when the door slides open, the elevator across from me doing the same to reveal Georgia struggling with a similar number of bags.

When she notices me, she too falls into a fit of laughter. People are looking at us, wondering what's so hysterical, but we just keep laughing, fully amused at this moment.

"Stop laughing," Georgia pleads, leaning over. "I've pushed three kids out of my vagina. My bladder control isn't what it used to be."

A man makes a disgusted face, skirting past her like she might pee on his shoes.

Unfortunately for her, this only makes me laugh harder.

Still giggling, we do our best to pull ourselves together enough to move away from the elevators.

I wipe tears from my eyes, hiccupping from the laughter.

Somehow, we manage to make it to a table and set down all our bags. I ask her what she wants and go off to get our food so she can babysit the bags.

When I return, she's tapping away at her phone but quickly sets it aside. "Sorry, I wanted to check in on Michael and he was scolding me for worrying. He assures me that things are going great."

I shake my head, stifling a laugh. "I wish we could see them all right now."

But truthfully, between all three guys, things shouldn't be going too bad. The girls are pretty easy—my two and Georgia's youngest—it's Georgia's two boys that are a handful.

Scouring through my purse for hand sanitizer, I drop some onto my hand and then Georgia's when she holds hers out for some.

"This is so nice," Georgia says, forking a piece of chicken. "I can eat without a kid chanting Mom over and over again." She closes her eyes, savoring the moment.

I point my fork at her. "Or being asked if they can have some."

Her eyes pop open. "Oh, that too! Do you know I picked up a sub on my way home from work one day and went to the bathroom when I first got there. By the time I came out, my sandwich was gone." With a shake of her head, she sighs. "Those boys eat everything. I don't even want to think about when they're teenagers." She smiles to herself, and adds, "But God, do I love them anyway."

I would never tell Georgia, but when she got pregnant with my first nephew, I was a tad worried. Georgia is a great person, but I never would've labeled her the motherly type. I honestly figured she'd never have kids. But she's truly one of the best moms out there, and I know she'd do anything for her kids. It's brought out an unexpectedly soft side of her.

"Anyway," Georgia says, turning her attention back

to her lunch, "is there anything you'd like me to bring for Thanksgiving? Listen, I know I'm not the best cook, but I'm sure I could whip up something halfway decent."

For Thanksgiving, Thayer and I will be hosting everyone at our house, and when I say everyone, I mean it. His parents are coming in, his brother, Caleb, Georgia and her family, and even our neighbors Thelma and Cynthia.

I love it, though, having everyone together. After everything, losing Forrest and my mom, it taught me the value in appreciating the people around you. Time is not replaceable.

I mull over her question. "How about the green bean casserole? You make it better than I do. Yours tastes more like Mom's."

Like always whenever I think of my mom, there's a momentary drop in my stomach. I miss her so much. There's this constant dull ache inside me that I've had to learn to live with. Certain things make that dullness grow to an intense throb, like holidays, or birthdays, or even something simple like wanting to pick up the phone and call her, then realizing I can't do that.

A wistful look steals over Georgia's face, and I wonder if she's feeling similarly to what I am. "I do?"

I give a half-laugh. "It's so much better when you make it than when I do."

She gives a short nod and smiles. "Yeah, sounds great. I can do that."

We finish up our meal and throw away the trash before the two of us take one look at each other and burst into laughter again, somehow already knowing the other is going to make the exact same request.

"Home?"

I loop my arm through Georgia's laying my head against her shoulder as we make our way to the elevators. "I thought you'd never ask."

CHAPTER SIX

Thanksgiving

Chaos.

That's the only word that comes to mind when Georgia's kids and mine run screaming through the kitchen chasing Winnie in an attempt to put a bandana decorated with turkeys around her neck. But she's not having it.

Binx peeks at me from the top kitchen cabinet, as if daring me to give away his position. I'm not about to rat him out.

"Order up," Thayer jokes, pulling a casserole dish of stuffing out of the oven and setting it on a trivet. With so many people gathered for the holiday, we're dishing everything up on the island, buffet style. Across the island, Laith rubs his hands together in eager anticipation.

"Can I get a plate yet?"

"No," Thayer gripes at his younger brother. "Some dishes are still warming. Be patient."

"What about just a nibble?" He holds up his thumb and index finger a centimeter apart.

"*No.*" Thayer looks ready to throttle his brother. There are some things you never outgrow as siblings, and Laith pestering his older brother is one of them.

Laith looks over at me and winks. "Annoying him is so fun," he mouths, having read my mind.

Somehow, I always forget how similar the brothers look

until they're both in front of me. Same wavy brown hair, except Laith has no streaks of gray yet, same eyes and mouth shape. Laith's nose is slightly crooked from a break when he was younger but even so, their noses are similar. The biggest difference between them is behavior. Thayer's much more serious, whereas Laith is always cracking a joke at something, eyes shining with silent laughter.

Once all the dishes are out and ready for everyone, Thayer dips his chin at Laith to finally grab a plate.

"Sweet." Laith rubs his hands together, then cups them around his mouth. "Hey, everybody! Food's ready!"

Steps are heavy against the hardwood floors as everyone makes their way into the kitchen. I think all of us are more than ready to eat.

"Kids," I call, crooking a finger. "Come on over here and sit down. We'll bring plates to you."

The kids reluctantly sit down at the small picnic table we bring out for occasions like this. I've already placed their drinks on it and now wait for it to calm down so I can get their plates, but I notice Thayer has already started on it and join him.

"Hey." I bump his hip lightly with mine. "Everything smells amazing."

He smiles down at me, placing a quick kiss on my forehead. "Don't act like you didn't cook half of it."

I roll my eyes playfully. I've never done that well with compliments. I'm not sure at this point if I ever will. It's much easier for me to give others credit than to accept it for myself.

"Oh, gosh, are you two making plates for the kids?" Georgia sighs, running her fingers through her hair. "I was going to get them, I swear."

"Don't worry about it," Thayer says before I can speak, "I

was making plates for Seda and Soleil anyway."

There's a look he gives then. It's just a split-second flash of icy-hot *pain*, and I know he's thinking of Forrest. He clears his throat, focusing on the task at hand.

I never know what to do when this happens. Frankly, I don't think there's anything I can do or say. This isn't the kind of thing you can make better with a hug or pretty words. Losing someone is always hard. Grief never goes away, but the loss of a child? Just the thought of something happening to one of the girls makes me want to throw up. It's no wonder Thayer was in the state that he was after Forrest's passing. I'd probably have been in far worse shape.

When I look over at Georgia, she's giving him a sympathetic look. I wonder, if we hadn't lost our mom, if we would've missed it—that look he gave. But when grief lives in your heart it's easy to recognize in others.

I place my hand on Thayer's back. "Let me finish this. I need you to check the garage for more paper towels. We're out in the pantry."

He jerks his head in a nod, disappearing quickly, and that's how I know I was right to give him a moment on his own.

"Should you go talk to him?" Georgia asks in a small voice, hands fluttering at her sides ready to take over if I give the word.

"No," I sigh, looking in the direction he disappeared. "He just needs a moment alone."

"All right."

By the time I have plates in front of all the kids and am working on my own, Thayer returns with the paper towels and stocks them in the pantry.

"Thanks," he whispers in my ear, in passing.

I just give him an understanding smile in return.

We finally join everyone at the dining room table and as tiring as the holiday has already been with visitors and cooking and just the typical insanity, I wouldn't have it any other way.

"Is there any chance we can convince you two to bring the girls and visit for Christmas?" Thayer's mom asks innocently.

Caleb is further down the table, beside Thelma and Cynthia, but I can sense him go alert at the question. His shoulders tense, and he almost curls inward like a turtle hiding in its shell. I think he stops breathing altogether as he strains to hear what we'll say.

"No," I tell her, wiping my fingers on a napkin. "I'm sorry, but we'll be staying here. Maybe we can come over spring break? Or summer vacation if it works for everyone's schedule?" I suggest.

I hope I'm not coming across as rude by dismissing her desire to spend Christmas with them, but there's no way I could ever do that to Caleb. I know it would crush him not to see Seda on Christmas day. Thayer's parents have never really understood Caleb's involvement with Seda since she's not his by blood. They don't realize that being a parent is so much more than what's in our DNA. Caleb shows up for Seda, and I can't say the same for a lot of blood-related parents out there. He deserves as much involvement as he wants.

"Oh." Her lips dip into a frown, her eyes shooting down the table to Caleb like she knows he's the real reason I'm turning her down. "That's too bad, but yes, perhaps we can work something out for then."

Beneath the table, Thayer gives my knee a reassuring squeeze to let me know he approves. I shoot him a small, grateful smile. He's always been so understanding and respectful of the situation.

Idle chat continues until Laith clears his throat loudly, demanding attention.

Everyone silences, our gazes swinging in his direction. He smooths his hair back, his eyes shifting around almost nervously in a very un-Laith-like gesture. He clears his throat again, this time unconsciously.

"Since we're all here, I thought this was as good a time as any to tell you all—"

"You have a girlfriend?" His mom interrupts, positively giddy.

"What? No, Mom, let me finish." He rubs a hand over his jaw, lips pursing with embarrassment. "I'm moving."

"Moving?" His mom, dad, and Thayer exclaim simultaneously.

"Yes," he says, more serious than normal for him, "I'm moving here."

"Here?" Thayer points to the table.

"Not into your house if that's what you're implying, but to Hawthorne Mills. I bought a house."

"You bought a house?!" Their mom shrieks. "Laith, why haven't you said anything?"

He shrugs. "I didn't think it was that important."

"Are you flying back to Colorado or ... ?" Thayer trails off for his brother to fill in the blanks.

"Yeah, I have to go back and plan the move, but—"

"Uncle Laith, you're moving here?" Seda shrieks from the kids table, having overheard him.

He grins at her. "That's right."

"Ahhh," she shrieks, running around to his side of the table. He scoots back just in time for her to tackle hug him. "Oh my God, we're going to have so much fun. Where did you buy a house? Is it close? Is it in this neighborhood? Can I ride my bike there? What about—"

"Whoa, kid, slow down there. No, it's not in this neighborhood, and no, you can't bike there. I mean, I guess you could, but I won't allow it, and neither will your parents, because safety is important." He taps her nose playfully.

"What brought this on?" their mom asks, still obviously flustered by this turn of events.

Laith shrugs. "It just felt like the right time to be near family."

"And what are your father and me? Chopped liver?" She says it playfully but the hurt in her voice is obvious to everyone, even Seda who scurries back to be with her sister and cousins.

"Aw, Mom, don't be like that. You know I prefer cold weather." He tries to shrug off her sadness. "I'd never be happy in Florida."

Her shoulders deflate with a sigh. "I know. You're right. I suppose this will be better anyway. We'll be able to see you more often."

Laith claps his hands together, looking a smidge relieved that she's not dragging out the conversation. "See, look at that. Total bright side."

"And," her eyes light up, "when we visit, we can stay with you. Thayer and Salem already have a full house without us."

The comment is innocent, and we do have a full house, but I can't help thinking of Forrest who should be here with us, and the baby I so desperately want. I lower my eyes to the table, stomach slightly queasy. Guilt settles inside me, feeling ashamed for even being upset. I have two beautiful, healthy girls. That should be enough. It is enough. But it doesn't change the fact that my heart yearns for another child.

"Oh no, Mom, surely you don't want to stay with me. You always say I'm too loud and brash. Thayer's your favorite, remember?" Laith rambles in panic, nervously running his fingers through his hair.

Both parents dissolve into laughter, amused over Laith's reaction, and conversation turns to other things.

As the evening winds down, food is sent off with guests, and the kitchen is clean once more, I find myself being so grateful for these people and this life. It hasn't been easy. I've gone through things no person should ever have to face, but because of those things it makes me even more thankful to have what I do now.

Thayer's parents have gone to bed, the kids are tucked in, and it's just the two of us in the kitchen when he turns the music on and pulls me in close.

"Dance with me," he murmurs in my ear. It's not a question.

Somehow, unconsciously, the quiet intimacy of dancing in the kitchen after a long, tiring day has become our thing. That thing that brings us together again, centers us, reminds us that while chaos can be overwhelming, it doesn't last.

But this—each other—does.

I lay my head on his shoulder, listening to the steady beat of his heart.

I am safe and I'm home.

CHAPTER SEVEN

Sunshine Cupcakes has been transformed into a winter wonderland. The front window boasts fake snow with a little village that I salvaged from the store when it was still filled with the antiques my mom sold. Every year when we put it up, it makes me smile and feel like there's still a part of her that's very much here in this space. A Checkered Past Antiques was her special place, that thing she had that was all her own. The thought of getting rid of the store had made me sick. I'm glad it all worked out in the end.

I adjust the specialty display. It's currently showcasing our Christmas cupcakes—things ranging from a snowflake design to a wreath.

"It looks perfect," Hannah tells me, sliding a tray of fresh chocolate cupcakes into the case. "If you keep messing with it, you'll never be happy."

I know she's right, but it's the perfectionist in me. I can't leave it alone.

"It's almost there." I shift the wreath cupcake just a smidge. "Ah, see. It's perfect now."

She comes around the counter to look. She cocks her head this way, then that. "Oh my, yeah, that millimeter made *all* the difference in the world."

I mock-frown at her blatant sarcasm. "Don't make fun of me."

She bursts into laughter. "Then stop being so ridiculous."

She heads into the back for more cupcakes while I check the time. It's close enough to opening time that I go ahead and unlock the door, switching the sign on the door.

Hannah takes over front counter duties while I join Susanne in the kitchen to finish frosting all the cupcakes we had baked in the early morning hours.

That's the hardest part of this job—not only am I running a business, but I have to be up at the ass crack of dawn to start baking. It's worth it, though.

Susanne smiles at me when I enter. I wash my hands and pick up an already prepared icing bag. Susanne is hard at work on a custom order of fifty cupcakes for a superhero themed birthday party, so I focus on finishing up our usual stock for the store.

Once I'm in the zone it takes me no time to finish up the cupcakes and send them out front to Hannah.

"Oh." I startle when I find Laith chatting with Hannah. "Hi, Laith, I didn't know you were stopping in." He hasn't flown back to Colorado yet, instead finishing up contracts on his new place while he's in town. He still hasn't told any of us exactly where it is, but claims he's keeping it a surprise.

"I thought I'd stop in while I'm out. I can't say no to cupcakes."

I shake my head at him. To Hannah, I say, "He can have whatever he wants, on the house."

"In that case," he rubs his hands together, "I'll take the lot." The last part comes out in a bad impression of a British accent.

I hold up a finger. "One. And Hannah?"

"Mhmm?" She hums, turning away from him to face me. Hannah's cheeks are tinged pink and there's a sheepish smile crawling up her lips like I've caught her doing something she shouldn't.

He's studying my employee way too much for my liking. The last thing I need is for Laith to put the moves on Hannah and cause me to lose my employee.

"Watch out for Laith. He's full of shit."

"Aw, Salem!" Laith calls out after me, saying something more that I don't hear as I disappear into the back.

I'm sure he's waxing poetic to Hannah now all about how wonderful he is.

"I need to look over some paperwork. I'll be in my office if you need me."

Susanne gives me a nod, so I know that she's heard me, but continues frosting with her reading glasses practically falling off her nose.

I hate this part of running a business—all of the paperwork and bookkeeping, but it's a necessary evil. I tend to try and work on it for an hour or two every day I'm at the store just to stay on top of things. It's not just the bookkeeping I have to keep up with after all. Making sure we have enough ingredients on hand is important. Once, early on when I first opened, we ran out of sugar. How does one run out of *sugar* at a cupcake shop? By not keeping track of things, that's how.

Now, I make sure to keep up with inventory and all the other little details.

I haven't been working nearly long enough when my phone begins to ring. I'm tempted to ignore it, but I realize that it's possible that one of the girls' schools is calling.

When I look at the screen, though, it's not the school. It's my doctor's office. My heart drops to the pit of my stomach.

"Hello?" I answer, hoping whoever is on the other end of the line doesn't notice the slight shake in my voice.

"Hi, is this Salem Holmes?"

"Yes, it is."

"We had an appointment open up with Dr. Carter tomorrow. She's not your usual gynecologist, but you were next on our list to call if someone canceled and wanted to give you the option."

I don't hesitate. "Yes, I'll take it."

She gives me the details and I write it all down. My handwriting is shakier than normal as I scribble down the information on a piece of scrap paper.

"We'll see you tomorrow," she says before hanging up.

I let out a deep breath, burying my face in my hands. Nerves make my stomach somersault. It'll be good, to be seen by a doctor sooner, to maybe get some answers or at least some sort of understanding. But it's incredibly terrifying to think about the answers I might get.

I have two beautiful daughters, I remind myself. *An amazing husband. A great life.*

No matter what comes of this, it'll be okay.

CHAPTER EIGHT

I didn't tell Thayer about the appointment.

Now that I'm sitting in the waiting room all alone, I'm wishing I had, but I had wanted to handle this on my own. In hindsight, it was a ridiculous idea, and I know he'll wish I had told him. But there's been a nagging thought in the back of my mind. One I've done my best to bury and never utter aloud—too terrified to even voice the possibility.

Cancer.

My mom was relatively young when she got breast cancer the first time. Still young when it came back and took her from this world.

I'd be lying if I didn't admit to that thought plaguing my mind, along with things like ovarian cancer, or maybe even just a benign cyst.

I feel a single tear cascade down my cheek.

Don't get me wrong, I would love to have a third child, but when the tests kept coming back negative over the last year, I didn't think anything of it at first. Then, I started to wonder if there was something more. Something deeper.

The thought of leaving my girls motherless is terrifying.

And Thayer? Who's already had to live through such unimaginable grief?

I can't imagine what that kind of news would do to him.

My stomach roils with the very thought of it. I close my eyes, counting backwards from twenty in an effort to get control of myself.

By the time my name is called, I've worked myself up into an unimaginable tangle of nerves. Thankfully, I do a good job of not showing it on the outside.

The nurse gets my weight, then takes me to a room where she checks my temperature and blood pressure. She inputs all the information into her laptop then asks me the usual series of questions before she finally asks the most important.

"What brings you in today?"

My fingers shake slightly, and I clasp them together in my lap. Her eyes follow the movement, and she gives me a small, reassuring smile.

"I ... um ... my husband and I, have been trying for another baby, and I haven't gotten pregnant yet. We've been trying for a year, maybe a little more. We started with that whole mindset of we're not trying, but we're not preventing either, which I mean ... that's like total bullshit, because that's definitely still trying ... " I swallow thickly, tucking a stray hair behind my ear. "Anyway, it hasn't happened, and it happened fairly quickly the other times and I ... " Oh God, I'm getting choked up in front of this woman I don't know. I feel a tear, then another, slide down my cheek.

She passes me a tissue box with a sympathetic smile. She probably deals with this kind of thing daily. "It's okay. Take your time."

I dab at my eyes, taking a few deep breaths to calm and center myself.

"My mom," I begin, clearing my throat in an attempt to gather myself. "She ... uh ... died a few years ago, from cancer. Breast cancer. I guess I can't help but be worried that maybe there's something more serious going on here. I haven't felt any lumps or anything like that," I hasten to add. "It's just been a worry, you know?"

The nurse jots down some notes on her computer, asks a few more questions, and says the doctor will be in shortly.

It feels like hours pass before the doctor enters in the room, which only allows my nerves to ratchet up to an all-time high.

Dr. Carter is a tall woman, probably in her forties, with kind eyes that give me the smallest bit of relief.

"Hi, it's so nice to meet you, Salem." She extends a hand to me, and I shake it. "Laura was telling me about some of your concerns, so we'll start with a basic exam, and I want to do blood work on you. It'll take a few days for that to come back, since I'll be sending it to an outside lab. I promise I'll call you as soon as I know the results, okay?" She gives me a reassuring smile and pat on my hand.

Her kindness, the pure gentleness, in the way she interacts with me has a few more tears slipping out of my eyes. I am a complete and utter wreck. Bless her for not judging me.

"That would be great. Thank you."

"All right," she says, pulling out the stool. "Let's get started, shall we?"

CHAPTER NINE

"Look at all the pretty lights, Sol!" Seda points, trying to get her little sister to pay attention to the Christmas lights out the car window.

Thayer shoots me an amused smile. His left hand is wrapped around the steering wheel, his right resting on my thigh. In the back of the car, are the girls—obviously—and then Caleb squished into the third row of the SUV. When we said we were going to drive around to see the lights, he asked to go but that meant being squeezed into the back. He hasn't protested once. That's just how he is as a person. He wanted to be with Seda, and that was all that mattered to him.

"Santa's on that roof! See?"

I look behind me and see that Soleil is still not paying much attention. Her eyes are heavy, fighting sleep.

Seda finally sighs in exasperation and just enjoys looking around on her own. It's sweet for her to try, but Soleil almost always falls asleep in the car within five-minutes of leaving the house.

As nice as looking at the decorated houses is, that's not our real destination. There's a park about forty minutes away that puts on a light show where kids can meet Santa. We're only looking at the decorated houses for now since that's the excuse we used with the girls. I know Soleil will perk up once we reach the park and she can meet Santa.

When we leave the neighborhood behind, I expect Seda

to ask where we're going, but she doesn't say a word until we're turning into our destination.

"Whoa, what is this place? Are those dancing penguins?" she gasps, practically vibrating in her seat at the giant light up penguins that move somehow.

Thayer rolls down his window, letting the Christmas music that's playing through the park drift back to us. "Yeah, kiddo, I think they're dancing."

"This is so cool. Daddy, did you know we were coming here?" she asks Caleb.

"No, I didn't," he replies with amusement.

I look back at him with an apologetic smile. "When you asked to tagalong, I couldn't spill the beans in front of the girls." I did text him, but he must not have checked his phone. Oh, well.

He laughs, amused. "I get it. This looks fun."

It takes Thayer a little bit of time to find a parking space. I guess we're not the only ones who decided to come out tonight to see what this was like. When he does park, Soleil comes awake with an annoyed squawk. Poor girl likes her sleep.

Piling out of the car, Thayer grabs the stroller from the back while I get Soleil out of her car seat.

It's been a few days since my appointment, and I haven't heard anything back yet. I'm trying not to stress about it. I still haven't said anything to Thayer. I figure I've kept my mouth shut up until now, I might as well stay quiet until I get some answers. Hopefully tonight will be a good distraction.

Once Soleil is strapped into her stroller, we all head toward the entrance where Thayer pays for the tickets.

"Mom!" Seda cries excitedly. "That sign says Santa is here! Does that mean I get to meet him? I have to tell him what I want." She jumps up and down, joy lighting up her sweet face.

I suppress a laugh at how adorable her excitement is. I hope she believes in Santa for a good while longer, because I sure will miss this. I'll still have it with Soleil, but there's something so fun about them believing together, those twin faces of wonder and excitement.

"You get to meet him."

"Ah!" She jumps up and down, then bends over to Soleil. "Did you hear that, Sol? We get to meet Santa!"

"Santa!" Soleil cries with matching excitement, her chubby hands waving manically. "I love Santa!"

"Which way do we go first?" Seda asks, pointing in every direction. I'm not sure how she doesn't end up dizzy from her spinning. "There's so much to see! So many pretty lights! Don't you love the lights?" She crouches down, hands on her knees to speak to her little sister.

"Lights so pretty," Soleil replies, eyes big and round with wonder.

"It all loops around together," Thayer explains, ruffling Seda's hair. She reaches up to fix it, sticking her tongue out at him in the process. He chuckles in response. "We'll see it all, don't worry."

We start our trek through the magical park. It really is beautiful with a multitude of holiday scenes.

"Let me out," Soleil demands, tugging on the straps of the stroller.

Thayer looks at me, arching a brow in question. I sigh. "If she runs off, you're the one chasing her."

He laughs, shaking his head. His nose has turned red from the cold, his beanie tugged low over his ears. "Deal," he agrees, letting her out of the confines of the stroller.

I take over pushing it, so he can deal with the toddler who likes to turn into a runaway every chance she gets. She's surprisingly fast for having such little legs. I talked about getting a leash for her, but Thayer laughed so hard over the suggestion that I dropped it.

Caleb falls into step beside me while the girls and Thayer get ahead of us.

"Are you having fun?"

He glances my way at the question. "Yeah, this is nice, but you know I'm always down to do anything with the girls."

Even though he's not accusing me of anything, I wince anyway. "I would've said something to you sooner, but you had said you'd be in Boston all week. I wasn't trying to leave you out."

"Hey," he says, grabbing my wrist so I'll stop walking. "I'm not mad. That thought never even crossed my mind."

"I never want you to think I'm purposely excluding you. That's all."

I'm glad Caleb is who he is—that he's kind, caring in a way most people aren't. But that doesn't mean it wouldn't be so much easier if he was a bad guy.

"I don't. Promise. You don't need to worry about me."

But I do. Even after all these years I worry about him. I know I broke his heart and until he finds someone, a love like I have with Thayer, I think I'll always feel guilty. Who knows, maybe even after that. Not that I regret our divorce. Thayer is the love of my life, and Caleb is owed more than the small portion of my heart I had left to give, but everyone deserves that once in a lifetime love.

Up ahead, I hear Seda. "Ms. Bloom!" she cries out her teacher's name. "Are you seeing Santa, too?"

Catching up with the others, I shoot a few sly glances Caleb's way to see if he has any sort of reaction to this new development. I swear there's a hint of a blush staining his cheeks, but with the ever-changing colored lights all around us, I could just be mistaken.

"Hi, Seda," her teacher greets. "Are you having fun?"

"So much fun!" She jumps up and down. I have a feeling she's going to crash when we get home.

Thayer scoops a wriggling Soleil into his arms, shooting a wink my way. My stomach dips at that look. I wonder if there will ever come a time when I don't feel like a giddy schoolgirl around him. I doubt it.

"Hi, everyone." Ms. Bloom waves, her eyes flicking over our group. She lingers over Caleb a second or two longer than the rest of us, then drops her eyes shyly. "Oh, um, this is my brother and sister-in-law and my little nephew."

The couple standing behind her waves. The little boy is probably around five or six.

Pleasantries are exchanged, and we part ways since they're on their way out in the opposite direction to what we're headed.

Caleb looks back over his shoulder at their retreating figures. "I ... uh ... I'll be right back."

He doesn't wait for anyone to reply before he's jogging after Ms. Bloom. A smile splits my face and I almost exclaim an excited "Yes!" out loud but manage to rein myself in.

Thayer looks from Caleb's retreating figure to me. "What's that about?" He arches an amused brow.

I give a shrug, unable to contain my smile. "Nothing ... for now. But who knows."

"Caleb and Seda's teacher? Now that would be interesting," he muses, setting Soleil back down.

"I just want him to be happy." I try to burrow deeper into my coat to fight against the cold. Snow is beginning to swirl around us. Despite my gloves, I lost feeling in my fingers a while ago.

Thayer wraps an arm around my shoulders, both of our eyes on the girls ahead of us. They haven't made it too far from us, captivated by a section of lights that are princess themed. Seda is bent down to Soleil's ear level, telling her something while pointing at one of the princesses.

"I know you do." He brushes his lips lightly against my cheek. I shiver from the warmth of his lips against my wind-chilled cheek. "That's one of the things I love the most about you—even if at times I wanted to kill the fucker for ever having the privilege to touch you." I can't help but laugh, even though I know he's serious. "The way you care about people is a beautiful thing, Salem. He'll find his person one day. Maybe it's her or maybe it's someone else."

I lace our fingers together, laying my head against the side of his arm as we walk.

"Hey, sorry about that," Caleb says, catching up with us as we finally near the line to meet Santa.

"What was that about?" I ask curiously, my smile amused.

He ducks his head, grinning down at his shoes. "Nothing."

Thayer barks out a laugh. "Did you get her number?"

Caleb clears his throat. I can't tell if his cheeks are red from the cold or if it's an actual blush. "Maybe."

"Mom, Dad, Daddy! Look! I can see Santa." Seda points excitedly as we round a turn in the line that shows the setup they have for photos. Santa sits in a large red velvet chair with a light scene decked out behind him that depicts elves in Santa's Workshop. "Oh, I'm so excited. Aren't you, Soleil?"

Soleil nods, her thumb stuck firmly between her lips. I cringe to myself, wondering where all her wandering hands have been before she shoved her finger in her mouth. I tug her thumb from her mouth, rubbing her hands with hand sanitizer.

When it's finally the girls' turn, Seda takes her sister's hand and sprints up to Santa Claus, helping her sister onto his lap before joining him. She immediately launches into what she wants for Christmas, then brings tears to my eyes when she tells him what Soleil wants. Those tears spill over when she asks if he can deliver a present to her brother in heaven.

Kids. I swear. They truly have the purest of hearts.

Beside me, I can tell her request is getting to Thayer. He clears his throat, covering his mouth with his hand.

We've done our best to keep Forrest a present topic in our house. The girls deserve to know about their older brother. It's not something we try to shove on them too much in fear of them resenting Forrest, not that Soleil understands it much yet, but it's important that he not be forgotten.

Clearing his throat, Thayer utters a gruff, "I'll be right back," and disappears toward our right where the food stalls are. I watch him go. I want to go after him, to provide comfort in some way, but deep down I know that's not what he wants or needs right now.

Caleb steps up in his place, sympathy written plainly on his face. "I can't imagine how he feels. I don't even want to think about it."

I say nothing, because really, what is there to say? The grief that Thayer carries around is unimaginable. He deserved so much more than this. Forrest deserved more.

But life isn't always tied up in a pretty, little bow.

That's the most unfortunate part.

No one is guaranteed smooth sailing.

The girls finish up with Santa, running back to Caleb and me. I pay for the photos with instructions on where to pick them up on our way out of the park.

Caleb crouches down to Seda. "Piggyback?"

She giggles excitedly, hopping onto his back. Her arms twine around his neck as he stands. Scooping up Soleil, I strap her back into the stroller. She fusses a little, but she's tired enough that she gives up quickly.

"Where's Dad?" Seda asks, head swiveling in search of him, as we start down the next part of the path.

"He needed a moment."

"Oh," she says, sadness in her voice. "Is it about my brother?" I nod. Seda's intuitive, especially when it comes to anything related to Forrest. "Is it because I asked Santa to take a present to him?"

"Yes," I answer honestly. "It meant a lot to your dad that you did that." I don't want her thinking her request was anything bad because it's not. "Sometimes when people are really happy, it makes them cry." I reach up with a finger, tapping her nose.

Her lips downturn. "I don't like for Dad to be sad."

"He's not, baby, I promise."

She doesn't look like she believes me. I'm sure he is a little sad, but sadness isn't always a bad thing. It's an echo of our love for a person.

Thayer eventually meets back up with us before we reach the end of the path, giving each of the girls a cake pop decorated like one of Santa's elves. Seda takes hers with a quiet thank you, still subdued with worry that she's upset him despite what I told her. Soleil on the other hand, stuffs the whole cake pop in her tiny mouth.

"Aw, Sol. Careful." I bend down, plucking some of the dessert from her mouth. Something I learned quickly when I had my first baby is that you have to get used to dealing with another human's slobber. She chews what's left in her mouth, then opens up like a baby bird for more.

By the time we make it back to the car, she's finished the rest of her cake pop.

Once the kids are securely in their seats, we make the drive back to Hawthorne Mills.

It doesn't come as much of a surprise when both girls fall asleep on the way back. Christmas music plays softly in the background, Thayer humming along to it while he rubs his thumb in gentle circles where he clasps my hand.

Looking back at the girls and Caleb, I smile to myself.

Despite everything, we're so blessed.

Dawn always comes, shedding light on our darkest nights.

CHAPTER TEN

My arms are loaded down with supplies for the Christmas party at Seda's school. I might've gone a bit—okay, a lot—overboard on the things I needed to get. But I figure you can never have too many plates or napkins or cups or—

Yeah, I definitely should've reined myself.

The weight of the plastic bin I stuffed everything in disappears. I cry out, afraid that everything is about to fall over in the wet parking lot. But I quickly realize that's not the case.

I smile up at my husband who now holds onto the bin.

"I thought you couldn't make it." I'm more than a little excited to see them. I wasn't exactly looking forward to braving the other mothers on my own. Some of them are so ... judgmental.

"Like I was actually going to miss Seda's party. I rescheduled."

Standing on my tiptoes, I press a kiss to his delectable lips. His beanie is pulled low, but his nose is still pink from the cold, highlighting a dusting of freckles still left over from the summer. His eyes crinkle at the corners.

Shutting the trunk, I lock up the car and we head inside, navigating our way to the gym.

The school is small, so they chose to have all the grades celebrate together, bringing tables into the gymnasium. With the kids still in their classrooms for the time being, the other parents take the opportunity to set up.

"Oh, perfect," one of the teachers says, coming over to us. "You're tall, and we need help hanging a few things," she says to Thayer. "Think you can help with that?"

"Sure. You good here?" He raises a questioning brow at me.

"I'm fine. Go on." I shoo him away.

Unloading the box of goodies I brought, I organize it by categories.

"I'm so glad you brought so much." I look up to find one of the moms—well, I assume she's a mom since she's not wearing a school badge—smiling at me. "We're already running low on supplies. I was worried we might have to run out for more, and we're short on time as it is."

I step aside so she can inventory what I've brought. "And here I thought I'd done too much."

"No, this is seriously great. You're a life saver." She clips her long, dark hair up. "I'm Bree by the way. I think my son is in class with your daughter. Seda, right?"

"Yeah, that's right."

"My son is Dawson. I think he has a little crush on your girl. He talks about her all the time." She gives a soft laugh, reaching for a pack of plates.

"That's cute."

And it is ... even if the idea of Seda dating one day terrifies me. It reminds me of a conversation I had with Caleb not too long ago, one where he asked me what I would do if Seda fell for a man older than her like I did with Thayer. It wasn't something I'd thought about, but I could tell it had been weighing on Caleb. I was honest with him, telling him I didn't know. The truth is her falling for an older man one day scares the shit out of me. My first instinct is to be angry at the idea, downright distraught at the fear of someone taking advantage of my little girl, but then I have to remind myself that wasn't the case with Thayer. Sure, I thought he was hot, albeit a bit of a grumpy bastard at first, but we fell slowly, naturally, together. Loving him was never choice. It was simply fate. How could I deny my daughter that same kind of feeling? That's a bridge I'll cross one day when she does fall in love. Whomever that might be with.

"If you want," Bree says, gathering up some of the plastic tablecloths I brought, along with more plates, "you can help Julia over there with sorting out the name tags."

Heading over to where she indicated, I introduce myself to the other parents before getting to work. We have less than hour to finish setting up and I know the kids will be restless, so there's no way we can delay it longer than necessary.

Luckily, enough parents showed up to volunteer that we manage to complete it just in time to open the doors.

The kids surge inside, oohing and ahhing over the decorations. Paper snowflakes the kids had made over the past few weeks in art class hang from the ceiling at varying intervals. The tables are organized by grade, with the teachers helping the kids to find the appropriate tables.

Thayer stands beside me, scanning the kids for Seda.

She spots us first, waving with wild excitement.

My gaze moves to Thayer, taking in how he lights up at her reaction. Thayer was meant to be a dad, there's no doubt in my mind about that fact. He loves his kids more than anything in the world.

"Hi, Dad!" she yells across the room. "Hi, Mommy!"

I wave back, struck with a sudden overwhelming emotion of melancholy. Everyone tells you not to blink, that it goes by fast. They're not wrong. In no time at all, she's grown into such an amazing kid. It won't be long until she's a teenager and then leaving us for college or whatever else she chooses to do in life.

Thayer clears his throat, his fingers twining around my wrist to bring my attention to him. "Sunshine, are you crying?"

"No." *I'm definitely crying.* He gives a soft chuckle in response. "It's just, look at her, she's so grown up and it scares me. I want it to slow down." I dab beneath my eyes, hoping Seda hasn't noticed, or she'll worry.

He pulls me in closer, wrapping his arms around me fully. He's ditched his coat somewhere, the sleeves of his blue Henley rolled up his muscular forearms. Inhaling his familiar scent, I let it flood my senses, instantly soothing me. Thayer always manages to make me feel better, even without saying a single word.

"She's going to grow up," he says softly, his mouth lowered near my ear. "It's scary, sure, but we can't spend so much time wishing our kids would stay little that we miss what we have now with them, because soon these will be the days we're longing for too."

He's right, which only makes me cry harder. "Sorry," I mumble, drying my tears on his shirt sleeve. "I don't know what's gotten into me."

But I think I do know. The stress and worry of waiting to hear back from the doctor is eating me up inside. I called the office this morning for an update and was told I might know something by this afternoon or tomorrow.

I'm so tired of waiting. As scary as it is, I just want an answer.

"Don't apologize, Sunshine. I love you even when you get snot on my shirt."

Sticking my tongue out at him he chuckles in amusement.

When all the kids are seated, the principal gets up to give

a short speech on the school year so far and how proud she is of the students. Then, it's time to serve the food and drinks. The kids are allowed to get up in sections, coming to each station to get their pizza and drink of choice.

It takes a while to get through all the students but once they're all seated one of the teachers pulls down a large screen and puts on the animated movie *Frosty the Snowman.*

"This is cute," Thayer remarks, spinning a finger through the air to encompass the gymnasium. "It's nice that they do all this for the kids. I'm glad I could come."

I am too.

I know getting to do these things with the girls means the world to him. After the loss of Forrest, I don't think he wants to miss out anything if he can help it. Sometimes we forget to prioritize the small things and by the time we realize, it's already too late.

Not that Thayer wasn't a present father with Forrest. He certainly was, but I think the things we look back on and regret the most turn out to be the little moments like this. They might not seem like anything, when in actuality, it's the world to your child. I know it still haunts him that he didn't just build that treehouse sooner.

When the food is gone and we've cleaned up the kids' tables, they work on a small craft project—wooden snowflake ornaments—while the movie continues to play in the background.

Thayer and I try to stay in the background, not wanting to interfere with Seda's time with her friends, but she waves us over.

"Mom! Dad! Come help me with my snowflake."

Thayer beams at her request. I wonder if he realizes he's

smiling so big. He might call me Sunshine, but he's the one who brings light to my world.

We squeeze our way in on either side of her. "Dad, will you help me add these?" She points to sapphire blue jewel-like stickers. "And mom can you put the glue on like this ... " She draws the design she wants with her finger so that I understand what she's asking. "Then I can sprinkle the glitter on."

"You got it, kiddo." Thayer ruffles her hair.

I pick up the Elmer's glue, drawing the design on her popsicle snowflake in what's hopefully the pattern she wants.

"How does that look?"

"Perfect. Great job, Mom."

I laugh at that comment, Thayer shooting me an amused wink.

Sticking her tongue out in concentration, she shakes teal glitter onto the glue, then taps her popsicle against the table to get rid the excess. "Do I get to go home after this?"

I fight an amused smile. "Yeah, the school day will be over."

"Sweet. I'm ready to bust out of this joint."

Thayer and I lock eyes over the top of her head, both of us trying desperately not to laugh.

It's true, what they say. Kids say the darndest things.

CHAPTER ELEVEN

Stifling a yawn, I set my book aside. Thayer hasn't come up to bed yet and it's getting late. Binx cracks an eye open from the bottom of the bed when I slip out from beneath the covers. Winnie snores peacefully in her cushion on the floor, all four paws sticking up in the air. I'm not sure even an earthquake would wake that dog.

Keeping my steps quiet so I don't disturb the girls, I go downstairs in search of him.

Light emanates from the kitchen. I find him sitting at the kitchen table, reading glasses perched on his nose. He studies the puzzle in front of him intently.

"Hey," I say softly, not wanting to startle him. He looks up from the puzzle. "I wanted to make sure you were okay?"

"Yeah." He sets down the piece he was trying to make fit, his gaze going to the time glowing on the microwave. "I didn't realize it got so late."

When we got home from Seda's school party, time was lost to making dinner, homework, baths, and bedtime. Something people tend to forget to warn you about when you have kids is how rarely you have time for yourself. It's not always easy to find time to recharge.

"That's okay." I tuck my hair behind my ear. "You can keep working. I just wanted to check on you."

He scoots the chair back but makes no move to get up. "Come here."

I hesitate only a second before my bare feet eat up the distance between us. I slip onto his lap facing him. His hands go to my ass, pulling me firmly against him. I gasp, rocking my hips into his. Tracing my fingers over the shape of his lips, I then play with the scruff on his cheeks. His eyes fall closed, letting me touch him as I please. Leaning forward, I place my lips softly over his.

"I love you," I murmur.

Three simple words.

I and love and you. Separate they're insignificant but put them together and they are everything—*he* is everything.

When I lean back, he opens his eyes. "I love you, too, Sunshine." He dives forward, cupping my cheek with the side of his hand, his fingers splaying behind my neck to hold me steady. I guess my featherlight kiss wasn't enough.

He grows hard beneath me, rocking his hip up into me until I moan. He smiles against my mouth, clearly pleased with how easily he works me up.

"That's it," he growls lowly, "let me hear what I do to you."

"Thayer." His name is a gasp and plea all in one. Leaning back from his touch, I tear my shirt over my head and drop it to the floor. I'm not wearing a bra since I was ready for bed, his eyes going eagerly to my exposed chest. He cups them gingerly in his hands. Bigger now, droopier too after having two kids, but Thayer's never made me feel anything less than beautiful.

Rubbing his thumbs over my nipples, they pucker beneath his touch.

"You're so perfect. How did I get so lucky?"

He must not be waiting for a response, because he dips his head down, swirling his tongue around my right nipple. My fingers tug on his hair, silently begging for more. His touch, his mouth, his cock. I just want him.

He moves his attention to my other breast, giving it the same treatment.

"God, you're so pretty," he croons in a husky rasp. "Are you wet already?" His eyes meet mine, my teeth biting lightly into my bottom lip. I give a slight nod. "Let me feel for myself."

His fingers slip beneath the elastic of my sweatpants. It takes him no time to find my aching, wet pussy. Dipping his fingers into my wetness, he brings them to my clit, rubbing in circles at the same time he kisses me again.

He brings me to an orgasm all too quickly, grinning as I fall apart on his lap.

Not giving me a chance to recover, he stands with me in his arms and sets my butt down on the table, pushing at my stomach for me to lie back while he tugs my pants down.

"Thayer. The puzzle."

He hooks his fingers into the back of his shirt, his stomach flexing when he yanks it off. It joins my clothes in a pile on the floor. "I don't care about the puzzle. I want to fuck my wife."

Oh, sweet Jesus.

I can certainly get on board with fulfilling that want of his.

Placing his hands on my thighs, he forces me to open up wider to him. He pulls me to the edge of the table, dropping to his knees in the process. Urging me to rest my legs on his shoulders, he slides two fingers into my aching pussy, rocking them in and out. Teasing me mercilessly when he knows I want more than that.

Then he swipes his tongue over me, my back bowing off the table. "Oh my God," I cry out, stretching my arms above my head. I rock my hips against his mouth, his tongue spearing my core while his thumb rubs against my clit. He's going to make me come again just like this. My body feels ultra-sensitive to his touch tonight.

He can sense it too as I wiggle against him. "Are you going to come just like this, Sunshine? Are you going to come on my tongue? I know you want to." He sucks my clit and that does it for me.

Slapping my hand over my mouth, I stifle my cries of pleasure. Thayer always knows what my body likes and needs without me even telling him.

"Fuck, you're such a pretty thing when you come." He stands up, pushing his pants down to free his erection.

I whimper with need at the sight of it. He chuckles, amused. "Give it to me," I beg, reaching between my legs to wrap my hand around his cock. "Fuck me hard. Please."

He smiles devilishly. "I really had planned to make you wait longer for my cock, but since my girl is asking so nicely ... "

He grabs my hand from around him and pins both of my hands above my head at the same time he slams into me. His mouth is over mine a second later, quieting my scream.

"You try so hard to be quiet," he murmurs in my ear, "but you never can. I need you to try, though. Can you try for me?"

I nod and he rises above me, his fingers digging into my hips using them as leverage to fuck me the way I want. Harder. Faster. I bite my lip, holding back sound. He's right, it's so hard to stay quiet.

"Do you think you can come again?"

"Y-Yes," I stutter, sweat dampening my brow. I'm embarrassingly close again already.

"Fuck, baby," he rubs my clit in a torturously slow pattern, "keep squeezing my dick like that and I'm not going to last."

"I can't help it," I admit on a whimper, grasping onto his

forearms like that'll keep me from floating away. "I-I—"

And just like that another orgasm rattles through my body, taking him overboard with me this time. He groans, collapsing over top of me as his lips seek mine. His strokes slow as he empties himself inside me.

I wrap my arms around him, and we stay like that for a long moment, as we both struggle to regain our breaths. My legs feel like jelly and I have no idea how I'm going to manage to make it back up to bed.

Thayer solves that problem for me by tossing me over his shoulder once he's recovered and carrying me up the stairs. We'll be up before the kids and can grab our discarded clothes then, so it's not a big deal.

Tossing me down onto the bed, I stifle a giggle.

He arches a brow. "Round two?"

With a nod, he pounces on me, and we start all over again.

CHAPTER TWELVE

I've been busy, so I haven't been running as much, and man do I feel it. Only two miles into my jog on the treadmill in the basement and my legs are feeling it.

I make a silent vow not to go so long without running again.

Sometimes it's hard to prioritize certain things when life gets in the way, but my runs have always been much needed "me" time.

When I hit mile three, I shut the treadmill off, grabbing my water bottle and draining half the contents in one gulp. I'm grateful the store is closed today. It means I can catch up on things I need to do at home, like wrap Christmas presents. Soleil's preschool has already shut down for the holiday while Seda still has a few more days. Thayer has a light workload today, just checking over some sites and drawing up plans for spring, so he took Soleil with him.

Wiping the sweat off my brow with a towel, I go upstairs to shower. There's no way I'll feel up to doing anything until I get this sweat off my body.

My phone rings while I'm in the shower. I don't think anything of it until I get out and see that it's a missed call from my doctor's office. Panic freezes me to the spot. Water drips off my body, pooling on the floor. It takes me a full minute to snap out of my frozen state. With trembling fingers, I set the phone back down, quickly pulling on a pair of leggings and sweatshirt before I call them back.

Sitting on the edge of the bathtub, I chew nervously at a hangnail. My heartbeat is a thunderous roar in my ears. My nerves have never been so taut. Dread is a heavy feeling in my gut.

When they pick up, my heart races as I say my name and wait to be transferred.

What if it's bad? What if I'm sick?

No! You can't think like that! It's going to be fine. It has to be.

Maybe I should've told Thayer, because right about now I feel like I'm going to faint, but then the nurse is on the line and I'm trying to listen to everything she's saying.

Blood work is normal.

Look great.

Nothing out of the norm.

Pregnant.

Wait. What? I couldn't have possibly heard her right. Perhaps I missed a few words and she asked if I'm still trying to get pregnant.

"Pregnant?" I repeat in a stunned voice. "Did you say I'm pregnant?"

She gives a soft, amused laugh. "Yes. According to the blood work you're about six weeks along."

If I wasn't already sitting, I'd certainly be on the floor by now. My free hand falls shakily to my still-flat belly. A baby. There's a baby inside me. It's what I've wanted more than anything all these months of trying, something I'd grown increasingly convinced wasn't going to happen. Another child, another perfect addition to our little family.

She says more, rattling off information and talks of

scheduling another appointment so she transfers me back to the front desk.

I'm stunned, still grappling with this news.

This is what I wanted, what we've wanted, but dammit if it hasn't managed to take me by surprise. I'd fully convinced myself that another child wasn't in the cards for us and that there was something wrong with me. I guess the timing wasn't right before and this new little soul was being far more patient than I was.

I rub my hand against my stomach, making an appointment for after the holidays when the receptionist comes onto the line.

It's not cancer. I'm not sick. There's nothing wrong with me.

But I am going to have another baby.

A little girl or boy to complete our family.

When I end the call, I let the tears stream from my eyes. I don't bother to wipe them away. I let them cleanse me of all the negative feelings that have been building inside me.

My first instinct is to call Thayer, but I hold myself back—not out of selfishness, but the desire to think of a special way to tell him the news.

This baby has been so wanted and conceiving was harder this time around, so I want to make the moment memorable for both of us.

Wiping my tears away, I stand up and try to get myself together while brainstorming how I'm going to tell him.

Lower lip wobbling, I look down at my stomach. "You're so loved already."

I know Seda is going to be ecstatic, and Soleil won't understand much right now, but I know with the way she loves her baby dolls she'll be obsessed with her younger sibling. I smile to myself, picturing bringing home our new baby and how the girls will love over them. I'm sure Soleil will want to kiss the baby over and over. And Seda? She'll be like a little mommy, helping me with the baby in any way she can.

My heart feels full—whole.

I'm ready for this next great adventure.

CHAPTER THIRTEEN

Christmas is right around the corner, and we've been slacking on the decorating front. I put up all of our stockings across the mantle, added garland to the stair railing, but there's one important feature we haven't gotten yet.

The tree.

Seda's been surprisingly chill about the fact that we haven't gotten one yet, but it could just be because she went with Caleb to get his and she got to help decorate that one.

But, late as it might be, we're getting a dang tree.

Thayer lifts Soleil onto his shoulders, her hands tugging at his hair. "Faster, horsey!"

"Careful, honey." He reaches up to loosen her hold. "That hurts."

Seda grips my hand, looking around. "All the good ones are taken already."

"I'm sure we'll find something." I give her hand a squeeze.

She's not wrong, though. It's a week before Christmas, so our options are lacking, but I think we can make do. The snow on the ground is icy and hard to trudge through, but I manage, making sure to hold on tight to Seda so she doesn't slip.

"That one's brown." Seda points out in a hushed whisper. "*It's dying.*"

It's only a *little* brown, but— "We're not getting that one."

"Maybe we should've gotten a fake tree from Target."

I sigh. I thought about it, that's for sure, especially since I have a feeling this won't be the only year time gets away from us when it comes to getting a Christmas tree.

"We could have," I agree as we follow behind Thayer, "but where's the fun in that?"

Seda looks up at me, gaze serious. "The fun is in the decorating, Mom. It doesn't matter if the tree is real or not."

"You have a point there."

"Hey," Thayer calls back to us. "It looks like there might be some options back here."

Seda sticks by my side as I cautiously navigate the icy, snow-covered ground. My boot starts to slip. I worry for a split second that I'm about to go down, but somehow Seda keeps us upright.

"Careful, Mom." She sighs in an exasperated way, like she's the parent and I'm the pesky child. "You don't want to fall and hurt yourself."

"No, I definitely don't." The last thing I need is a bruised butt.

We follow Thayer to where a few decent trees still lie in wait of a home.

"Which one do you think, girls?" Thayer asks Seda, then taps Soleil's hand so she knows he's talking to her too.

Seda lets go of my hand, stepping forward to inspect the three good choices we have. She taps her bottom lip with her index finger, taking this job seriously.

"This one looks a little crooked on top." She points to the one on the right. "See?"

I tilt my head to the side. It's subtle but it's there. "Cross that one off the list then?"

"I think so."

Hands on her hips she goes back and forth between the

middle and left ones. “This one,” she finally decides on the one in the center. “What do you think, Sol?”

“Dat one,” Soleil concurs, smacking her hands against Thayer’s head. He sighs, grabbing her hands so she’ll stop using his skull as a drum. He slowly lets her down from his shoulders, passing her over to me.

Settling Soleil on my hip, Thayer picks up the chosen tree like it weighs nothing and carries it to the front. The girls and I follow behind him. It doesn’t take long to pay and then he gets to work attaching it to the top of the car.

“Are we going to decorate the tree when we get home?” Seda’s eyes are wide, watching her dad fix the tree into place on the roof of the vehicle.

“Yep. I already brought the boxes of ornaments up from the basement.” It was a workout carrying all those up the stairs, not to mention trying to dodge Winnie and Binx in the process. Those two follow me everywhere. “Are you excited?”

She nods eagerly. “Can we make peppermint cupcakes too?”

“Sure. That’ll be fun.”

Even though I bake cupcakes all week, I never say no when she asks. Any time I can cook or bake with my girls is special. It’s one of the best bonding experiences. I’ve been baking with Seda since she was a baby. I’d put her up on the kitchen counter in her bouncer. I can still remember the way she’d kick her feet in excitement, the sweet little cooing sounds she’d make too.

“Mom?” She asks, voice wavering with worry. “Are you crying?”

I wipe away the tears. “Sorry.”

“What’s wrong?”

“Nothing’s wrong, sweetie.” I brush my fingers gently

through her hair. "Sometimes I just get a tad emotional at how fast you two are growing up."

"Oh. Well, don't be sad. I'm never going to leave you."

I laugh, knowing very well that one day she's definitely going to be leaving us.

Hands on his hips, Thayer takes a step back to assess how well the tree is aligned on top of the car. Double checking the straps, he nods to himself in approval.

Clapping his hands together, he turns to us. "All right, let's go."

***

Christmas music plays from the TV speakers thanks to the holiday music channel. I stretch up on my tiptoes to add an ornament we made when Soleil was a baby of her handprint. Seda and Soleil run around the couch, laughing and giggling, on a sugar rush from the hot chocolate Thayer made for all of us when we got back home.

Thayer's hand slides around my stomach, his thumb rubbing lazy circles against my skin where my sweatshirt has ridden up. I inhale a shaky breath thinking of the baby there that he doesn't know about yet.

I spent a few hours off and on, a few days ago, browsing the internet for a way to tell him that would be special. Memorable. I finally decided on having an art piece commissioned. I've been checking my email way more often than normal in hopes of seeing an early sketch.

"Let me get that." He slips the ornament easily out of my hand, sticking it onto the higher branch I was having trouble reaching.

I lean back into his chest, tilting my head to look up at him. "Thank you."

"What else do you need help with?"

I point to the box that's practically empty at this point. "Those are the last ones that need to get put up. As you can see, the girls did a great job on the bottom."

His eyes crinkle at the corners with a smile at the haphazard placement of ornaments that decorate lowest half of the tree. "It looks fantastic."

Both our eyes drift over to the couch where both girls have collapsed in a fit of giggles. Maybe they're finally crashing from the sugar rush.

Thayer adds the last of the ornaments to the sparsely decorated top of the tree, then gathers up the boxes to store in the basement.

"Do you girls want any snacks?" I ask, fighting my amusement at the way they both curl into the couch, eyes heavy. Seda shakes her head, Soleil too busy shoving her thumb in her mouth to answer me. "Should I put a movie on?"

I get two head nods in response. It doesn't take me long to put The Santa Clause on and then they're absorbed in that, the rest of the world fading away. Oh, to be a kid again at Christmastime. Not that I had the best holidays growing up, not with the kind of father I had, but there's still a feeling you get as a child that can never be replicated as an adult. I think it's a special time in your life when magic can be real.

On my way to the kitchen for some Diet Coke, I nearly bump into Thayer coming up the stairs.

"What are you doing?" I eye him suspiciously, my gaze lingering on the hand he holds behind his back.

He slowly walks toward me, then stretches that hand high

above our heads.

Mistletoe.

"Mistletoe," he says, a soft grin playing on his lips. With his free hand he tugs me closer. "You owe me a kiss, Sunshine."

I roll my eyes playfully, like kissing my husband is such a burden. Looping my arms around his neck, I stretch up on my tiptoes. Slowly, softly our lips meet.

I love this man so much, and I'm so incredibly lucky to have found him.

Our lips part and he kisses my forehead gently before lowering his arm with the mistletoe.

It's right there on the tip of my tongue to tell him I'm pregnant. I'm practically bursting at the seams to tell him. I bite down on my tongue to hold in the words, to wait, because I know what I have will be such a special way to give him the news.

"What?" he asks, no doubt noticing my racing thoughts.

"Nothing." I turn toward the kitchen for my Diet Coke. "Just thinking about how happy I am."

He follows behind me, sliding out a kitchen stool. "Really? Because it looked like you wanted to tell me something?"

"No." Somehow, I manage to keep my voice as light as possible. "Like I said, I'm happy."

My back is to him as I grab my drink, so he can't see the nervous face I make staring into the fridge. It doesn't seem like he suspects a baby, and luckily for me I haven't felt any sort of sickness. Yet, at least. It's not like I've had to worry about giving myself away because of running to the bathroom to throw up.

I take a sip of my Diet Coke, leaning my arms on the counter to face him.

His eyes are narrowed upon me. "You're definitely up to

something."

It's on the tip of my tongue to retort, "I am not." But I swallow down that response. Picking up my drink I turn away, heading to join the girls. "I don't know what you mean."

Suddenly he's there, hands on my hips. Backing me into the wall, he stares down at me with an amused smile. "You can never lie to me, Sunshine. Is it a Christmas present you're thinking of? Hmm." His nose glides against the skin of my cheek, trying to coax an answer out of me. "What did you get me?"

"Stop," I giggle, his beard tickling my neck. He only rubs the raspy, stubbly hair into me more, my laughter growing. "Okay, okay—yes, I was thinking about a present I have for you."

Mercifully, he stops. "You gonna tell me what it is?"

I press my lips together, shaking my head. "Tempting, but no."

He gives a good-natured sigh. "You're going to make me suffer and wait until Christmas?"

I smile up at him, my hand on his chest. "That's kind of the point of Christmas presents, Thayer."

He shakes his head like he can't believe I would dare do this to him.

"Yep." I pat his chest. "You'll just have to wait and see what Santa brings down the chimney for you."

His tongue slides out, moistening his lips. "Cruel, beautiful woman."

"You love me."

He smiles. "That I do."

He presses a slow, gentle kiss to my mouth. Standing on my tiptoes, I press up further into him, deepening it.

"No! No!" Soleil shoves her body into the middle of us, using her hands show pry us apart. "No kissy. Yucky."

Thayer chuckles, planting one last quick peck on my lips before he scoops up the little monster. "I thought you were watching a movie?" He tickles her tummy. "What are you doing in here?"

"Wanna snack."

"You want a snack?" He carries her over the pantry. "Show me what you want."

Of course, she wants a snack now. It's not like I asked her five-minutes ago or anything. Kids, I swear.

I join Seda on the couch, her body immediately snuggling into mine. "I love you, Mom."

My heart.

These are the moments I live for, the small in-between moments that in the overall landscape of life are so tiny, downright miniscule but it's where the sweetness is found.

"I love you, too."

Thayer joins us a few minutes later with Soleil wrapped around him and a bowl of grapes in one hand. I guess she decided on that for a snack then.

He sits down with her stretching his legs out, and she settles beside him, reaching eagerly for her bowl. He passes it over, then catches me watching them and winks.

I can't help thinking to myself how for so long I didn't think I was worthy of this. Of a good, happy life. That too much darkness from my past clung to me. I was wrong for ever thinking that, even if it's probably a normal thought for someone like me.

But here I am, on the other side with a family of my own and happier than I ever thought I could be.

Grateful.

I am so incredibly grateful to have weathered through the many storms tossed my way, because I know in my heart there are too many others who aren't so lucky.

CHAPTER FOURTEEN

Christmas Eve

The lights on the Christmas tree twinkle against the window, the only source of light in the family room. We can't risk any other light in case one of the kids wake up. It'd be absolutely disastrous if they found us playing Santa.

Thayer sets the last of the presents from the basement beneath the tree, turning to me to confirm that it is, in fact, all of them. His brow is arched in disbelief at the amount of presents.

"I promise that's it." I stick my hands up innocently. "I might've gone a bit overboard."

"A bit?" He looks around at all the stacks of presents, overflowing from beneath the tree, stacked on the side table, the chair, and even in front of the fireplace. Not *all* of them are for the girls. There's plenty of gifts meant for his brother and parents when we see them, Thayer himself, Caleb, my sister and her family, and even our nosy Thelma and Cynthia.

"There were lots of sales," I defend, hands on my hips. "And I've been buying things through the year so ... yeah." I scratch at the side of my nose, cringing a bit at the sheer volume of gifts. "I should've kept up with it better."

Next year I'll write it all down in a notebook or something.

Who am I kidding? I won't do that.

He cups my face. "You have a giving heart." Then with a

chuckle, he adds, "One that maybe gives too much. Not that the girls will complain."

"This is true." He kisses me quickly, letting go of my cheeks. "You make a hot Santa." I flick the end of the Santa hat he donned before we started bringing the gifts up from the storage room, I stashed them in. It's the best space for hiding gifts since I can lock the door with a key. Seda might be a good kid, but if given the chance I have no doubt she'd go snooping for her presents.

"Is this what gets you hot and bothered, Sunshine?" He points at the hat he dons, brows rising in surprise.

"You do. Not that you don't know that already." Swallowing thickly, I ask, "Can I give you a present now?"

It's been eating at me not to give him the art I had done when I got the finished piece yesterday. It came in just in time. I was worried it wouldn't make it but call it a Christmas miracle because it did. Luckily, I had already purchased a frame so once I had the art, I could slip it inside and wrap it.

Now, though, feels like the perfect time to tell him. We're less than an hour from Christmas day itself, and I want to tell him like this—just the two of us, so we can soak in the moment. We'll tell the girls tomorrow.

He gives me an amused half-smile. "What do you want to give me?" There's a hint of mischief in his tone, and I know he's hoping I have something of the sexy variety planned.

I push playfully at his chest. "You know I can't tell you. Hold on."

I carefully step around the presents, finding where I stashed this one behind the armchair. I wrapped it in icy blue paper with a silver bow.

He looks at it curiously as he takes the rectangular package and sits on the couch with it.

My heart begins to race. A mixture of nerves and excitement. Opening the edge of the paper, he eyes me curiously. I press my hands to my mouth in an effort to conceal my smile. But he knows. He *always* knows.

"You have me a bit nervous over what this might be, trying to hide that smile from me."

I drop my hands, schooling my features, and smooth my hands over my lap. "Just open it," I practically beg him.

Keeping this a secret from him has been one of the hardest things I've done.

He rips the paper off like I asked, letting it drop to the ground. Flipping it around, he studies the gift. His eyes scan over the watercolor painting of our family. Soleil sits on his shoulders, the two of us looking at each other. My belly round with our next baby. Seda's hand is grasped in mine, her head leaning against my arm. I couldn't leave out Forrest, though. He holds onto Thayer's leg, peeking around. A halo rests above his head.

"You added Forrest," he says, clearly choked up. "Look at him." He traces his finger over the shape of the little boy's face. "It's perfect. Thank you."

"There's more," I prompt, nudging his knee with mine, waiting for him to notice the bump. "Look closer."

He gives me a funny look before studying the painting more intently. His lips part the moment he notices, his head swinging so quickly in my direction I won't be surprised if he has whiplash.

"You're pregnant?"

I nod, tears flooding my eyes. Ugh, I wish I could make it through this without crying, but I knew it would be inevitable no matter my wishes. "Yeah, I am."

His eyes are wide with awe and surprise. He sets the framed art down slowly, putting his hands over my stomach in a protective, cradling gesture. "There's a baby in there?"

I put my hand over his. "There really is. I got a call that I could get an appointment with a different doctor, so I took it. I was worried that maybe there was something else wrong. I mean, my mom was relatively young when she got her diagnosis—"

He puts his hand on my cheek. "Oh, baby." Sadness that I'd keep my worries from him infuses his voice.

"I didn't say anything to you because I was scared, and I guess I wanted to live in this little bubble where no one else shared my fears. But I'm good. Healthy."

"And pregnant," he adds, laughing with excited disbelief.

"Yes," I give a small laugh, "that too."

"How far along?"

"Not much, about seven weeks now. I go back after the first of the year for another appointment."

He gives me a probing look. "I'm going this time."

I smile, not having expected less from him. "Definitely."

Sometimes I still have moments of sadness that he missed out on those things with Seda. But at least we got to do this together with Soleil and now this baby too.

"A baby," he says again softly, reverently. "We're going to have another baby. When are we telling the girls?"

I worry my bottom lip between my teeth. "I thought we could do it tomorrow after they open presents. Let them have their moment and then tell them."

He pulls me into his arms then, hugging me close. "I'm so happy, Salem."

I hug him back, clutching his shirt like he's a buoy keeping me from being adrift at sea. "Me, too."

"I love you." He kisses me. "I love you so much." Another kiss.

I smile at him, at this man who stole my heart and made it his. "I love you, too."

He kisses me again, then lets me go. Picking up the art, he looks it over again. "Thank you for including Forrest. He's ... uh ... he's a big brother again." He rubs a hand over his jaw, tears flooding his eyes.

His words pierce my heart. "You never have to thank me for that. Forrest is our family. He'll always be with us in some way."

I spent less than a year getting to know him, but it's safe to say Forrest left his mark on my life. He was the most special kid. There were so many things he never got the chance to experience. Seda and Soleil, too, will never know their big brother. Just because they know about him, and we keep his memory alive, it doesn't replace the real life experience they could've had with him.

He nods, clearly trying not to get emotional but a few tears escape anyway. "He would've been the best big brother, wouldn't he?"

"The greatest." I have no doubt about that. Forrest was an incredible, loving little boy. It's unfair that his life was cut short.

"He's happy for us. I feel that." Thayer taps his heart over his shirt. "God, I fucking miss him."

I wrap my arms around my husband's shoulders, letting him cry against me. Often, I've wished I could take his pain away, but then I wonder if that's a selfish thought because the hurt he's feeling is stemming from love—a deep, irreplaceable kind of love.

I know he's happy about the baby. I have no doubt about that, but I've learned with the loss of my mom that big life moments bring incredible sadness too when the ones you love are no longer there to share it with you.

And that's okay. You can be happy and sad at the same time; it doesn't mean you aren't thrilled about something. If anything, it means you treasure it more.

Thayer holds me tighter, and I press kisses to the top of his head, letting him feel what he needs to while I don't say a word. That's something else I've learned. Sometimes you don't need words. You just need someone to hold you—to know that no matter what, they're there for you.

CHAPTER FOURTEEN

Christmas Day

Thayer, Caleb, and I are already awake, having gulped down coffee as quickly as we could since we knew the girls would be scurrying down the stairs the moment they opened their eyes. I'm allowed to have a little caffeine while pregnant, and I knew I'd need it this morning.

"Did Santa come?" Seda hollers, her feet thudding against the stairs.

Soleil starts up a chant of, "Santa! Santa!"

They reach the bottom of the stairs, sprinting around the corner into the family room. Soleil nearly collides into Seda but catches herself just before a collision can happen.

"Ahhh! Look, he did, Soleil! See all the presents?" Seda turns around, bending to hold Soleil's arms.

The two of us watch from the doorway as the girls look around at the wrapped gifts in awe. We'll let them open everything from Santa and us first before we Facetime family so they can watch the kids open their presents from them.

"I wanna open," Soleil says, attempting to pick up one of the bigger boxes. She huffs and puffs through her attempt, blowing out her chubby cheeks. "Too heavy," she finally declares, throwing her hands up in irritation.

Thayer scoops her up, pressing a kiss to her cheek. "That's not yours anyway. Let's find one that says Soleil." He scans the piles that we purposely mixed up, so it takes Seda longer to open her presents since she's forced to search for her name. "Ah," he plucks up a smaller box, "here's one for you."

He plops down on the couch with her in his lap. She takes the box from him, tearing eagerly at the paper.

Tongue sticking out her parted lips, Seda searches for a package that sparks her interest.

Caleb and I join Thayer on the couch, watching as Seda finally settles on one. Sitting on the floor, she begins to unwrap it—much gentler than her sister. Her mouth pops open in awe when she sees what's beneath the paper.

"Thank you, Mom and Dad!" She holds up the box with wireless earbuds triumphantly. Setting it aside on the coffee table, she seeks out another package. Scooping one up, she hands it to me. "This says it's for you." She doesn't hesitate before she dives back in pursuit of her own.

Caleb leans back against the cushions, sipping his coffee.

Arching a brow, Thayer points to the gift in my lap. "Go for it, Sunshine."

I don't hesitate, tearing off the paper to find a set of my favorite skincare products. The stuff is pricey, so I definitely won't complain about having the set.

"Thank you," I murmur, leaning over to kiss his cheek.

He grins over at me. "Do I get a kiss with every present you open? I should you warn you, there's quite a few."

I shake my head at him. "You ... you ... I have no words for what you are." I wag a finger at him. All he does is laugh in response.

"Ooh, yay! I love this!" Seda holds up a case of art supplies. "Can I paint something later?"

"We'll see." I stifle a laugh of amusement. "Make it through all your gifts first."

Beside me, Caleb chuckles. "That might take a while." He motions lazily to the presents, which only grew when he arrived this morning.

"I know, I know," I chant, lifting my hands innocently in the air. "I did too much, but they're only young once."

Caleb leans further into the couch cushions. "I didn't say a word."

"Neither did I," Thayer echoes on my other side, helping Soleil open another present.

"Cheers to that." Caleb leans past me, mug extended to Thayer.

With a laugh, Thayer picks up his cup and clinks it against Caleb's. "Cheers."

***

The rest of the early morning passes with more gift opening before it's time for breakfast.

Leaving Caleb in the family room to play with the girls, Thayer and I head to the kitchen to start breakfast. As I reach for the handle of the refrigerator, his arm wraps around my middle, flipping me around.

"Wha—"

His mouth closes over mine, stealing the breath from my lungs. Hands on his chest, my fingers curl into his shirt, kissing him back. He smiles against my lips. "You're pregnant," he murmurs, softly, rubbing his fingers over my stomach.

"I am."

Resting his forehead against mine, he bites his bottom lip to hide his smile. "I'm so happy."

"Oh, shit." Caleb's voice breaks our little bubble. "Sorry, I didn't mean to interrupt."

I laugh as Thayer releases me. He straightens his shirt where my fingers wrinkled the fabric. "You didn't. I suppose we should tell you anyway?" I arch a brow at Thayer, and he nods.

Caleb looks between us curiously. I crook a finger, urging him to come over to us in case little ears are listening. We ended up deciding to wait and tell the girls on New Year's Eve.

"What is it?" Caleb whispers, looking around for any little ears that might be attempting to eavesdrop. "Is it a secret?"

"For now, it is," I say, voice hushed. It's hard for me to contain my excitement and Caleb's eyes light up with understanding before I even say. "I'm pregnant."

"Wow." He rubs his jaw, smiling. "Congratulations, guys."

I can tell he means it, but I also see the sadness in his eyes which breaks my heart a little. It was just a flicker, and only because I know him so well was I able to catch it. I know Caleb wants a family of his own one day—not that he doesn't have that with Seda, but with sharing her it's not a full-time gig for him. I know one day he'll find someone, the right someone, to share his life with. He deserves that more than anyone.

I reach out, grasping his arm lightly. "Have you been out with Ms. Bloom yet? What's her name? I feel terrible that I've never asked. I just never wanted to slip and start calling teachers by their first name in front of the kids, so they think it's okay to do that."

After we ran into Seda's teacher at the park light show I never followed up with him on what came of getting her number. It's one of those things that just slipped my mind with as busy as we've all been.

"No," he shakes his head, taking a step away, "we haven't.

I don't know that we will." He shrugs like it's not a big deal, but I feel like it is. She's the first person he's shown genuine interest in, in a long time.

"Why not?" I demand softly. Thayer detects the hint of worry in my tone, his hand settling around my waist. United, always.

Caleb sighs, running long fingers through my hair. "It's still the same issue of her being Seda's teacher, and with the tutoring..." He trails off, eyes dropping to the ground. "Seda spends a lot of time with her. I don't want her getting any more attached if things wouldn't work out. It wouldn't be fair."

"To her or you?" I counter.

Thayer pinches my side in warning to not keep pushing Caleb, but I can't help it. I see the way he holds himself back. I hope it's not because of me. I don't want to presume it is, because that seems awfully self-righteous.

Caleb's face scrunches like he might not say more, but instead he sinks into one of the stools, resting his head in his hands. He reminds me so much of that boy I fell for when we were teens. Something vulnerable and young in his expression.

"I don't have the time for a relationship."

I open my mouth to reply, but Thayer beats me to it. "There will always be an excuse not to pursue something. If you like her, what's the harm in one date? Get to know each other a little. There might not be anything there or you might be trying to throw away something great."

He mulls over Thayer's words. "I understand what you're saying. I'll ... I'll consider it." He nods to himself like it's decided.

It doesn't escape my notice that he didn't tell me her name, almost like he wanted to keep that tidbit of information to himself.

Thayer steps away, glancing down at his phone. "Laith says he'll be here in about five-minutes."

"Seda's going to be so excited to see him."

Laith asked us not to tell the girls he was flying in today for Christmas. With everything taken care of back in Colorado, he'll be staying with us until closing on his new house. I'm not sure he realizes what he's in for living in Hawthorne Mills. The nosy, tight-knit community isn't for everyone, and he tends to like to keep things to himself.

As if I've conjured her, Seda runs into the kitchen, a pair of Minnie Mouse ears on her head—a gift from her grandparents, and what I think is a not-so-subtle reminder to Thayer and me of our talk about coming to visit over Spring Break. I'm just glad his mom didn't give us too hard of a time over not coming for Christmas.

"Binx is trying to knock the ornaments off the tree." Her words are breathless from her run from the family room into the kitchen. "I tried to get him to stop, but he won't."

"He's probably wanting attention from me." Binx is the best cat ever, but there have definitely been times over the years as he's gotten older and our family has grown that jealousy has shown through. Since he's never been the kind of cat to mess with the Christmas tree, my bet is on him being needy.

Seda skips back to the family room, me following behind which leaves my husband alone in the kitchen with my ex-husband. I would shudder over the thought if they hadn't done such a good job of working things out between them. They're not best friends, not by a long shot, but they're ... something, and I guess that counts for everything in our weird dynamic.

Sure enough, Binx is trying to bat off the ornaments from the tree. I scoop him up, twirling away from the tree with him in my arms. "You don't need to do that." I kiss the top of his head. "You know better than that."

Sitting down, I curl my legs beneath me and snuggle Binx. My needy, sweet cat. Sometimes I wonder what would've happened if I hadn't found him that day so many years ago now. I think I might've needed him more than he did me.

Seda reaches over the back of the couch, petting the top of his head. "He really loves you."

"Animals gives us the best, unconditional kind of love."

She gets a small smile. "Can I have a pet of my own?"

I mull it over. "One day."

Her nose crinkles, hand never stilling from petting Binx. "Tyler in class says that when parents say that it actually means no."

I laugh, amused. "Well, in this case I do mean it. Of course, we'd have to ask your dad, but I don't see it being a problem."

She grins at me. "He's a pushover."

"Seda," I scold, but it loses any power thanks to the fact that I can't stop laughing. "Don't say things like that about your dad."

"What?" She shrugs innocently. "It's true."

This kid.

"What about me?" Thayer asks, appearing in the large archway leading into the family room. He bends, scooping Soleil into his arms. Somehow, she manages to keep a hold on her new favorite doll.

I'm saved from answering by the doorbell ringing.

"Who's that?" Seda asks me, hand stilling. "Uncle Laith!" She screams at an ungodly octave a moment later when he steps inside. Running from the room she nearly trips over a pile of opened presents in an effort to get to him.

He lets out an *oomph* sound when she collides with him. "Hey, kid," he greets. "Hi, everyone."

"How was your flight?" Thayer asks, shutting up the door to keep the cold out.

Laith winces. "If there ever was going to be a flight to make me throw up, it would've been that one."

"Oh, man." He claps his brother on the back. "Sorry about that."

Laith chuckles. "You weren't the pilot or the wind."

Caleb joins them in the foyer, greeting Laith with a handshake.

"How are you?" he asks me, shrugging out of his coat.

"I'm great." And it's true. I couldn't ask for a better Christmas. I have everything I could possibly want or need.

"Good, glad to hear it."

With his coat off, he bends down to give Seda a proper hug then ruffles Soleil's hair where she lays her head against Thayer's chest. Of course, her thumb is in her mouth.

"Are you hungry?" Thayer asks him. "I was just about to start breakfast."

"Starved." Laith rubs his belly for good measure.

I completely forgot about breakfast—is it too early to blame that on pregnancy brain?

It doesn't matter, though, not when the three guys head into the kitchen to cook. I'd be in the way at this point.

Soleil toddles toward me. I guess she didn't want to stay in the kitchen with the guys.

"Mommy, iz Christmas. I wuv Christmas."

She gives a dreamy sigh, using her chubby hands to help heave her body onto the couch with me. On her knees, she scoots closer and pets Binx. Her idea of petting at her age is more like smacking.

I grab her hand in a gentle hold. “Like this, Sol. You have to be soft.” I guide her hand to pet him the way she should. “If you can’t pet nicely then you have to leave him alone.”

She juts her lower lip at me, not liking that response. But once I release her, she pets him the way she’s supposed to. “Like ‘dis?”

“That’s perfect.” I kiss her chubby cheek. “You’re doing good, baby.”

She smiles at that, her teeth small and spaced apart still. It occurs to me then, that she won’t be my baby much longer. I knew this, but I don’t think the reality had quite sunk in. Now, it does. Soleil is going to be a middle child. Technically, both her and Seda will be middle children. It’s a weird thing to think about.

I heard that Krista, Thayer’s ex and Forrest’s mom, remarried about a year ago. I don’t know more than that, but I genuinely hope she’s doing as okay as she can be. I have no idea how she is now, but no one deserves what she had to go through. I hope she’s as happy as she can be.

“What you thinkin’ about, Mommy?”

Soleil’s sweet voice pulls me from my thoughts. “Nothing, baby girl.”

“Otay.” She lays her head on my chest, thumb finding her mouth. With a sigh, I tug her finger out. She growls at me in the way only a toddler can, shoving that thumb right back in.

We’re definitely going to have to work on the thumb sucking before it gets even more out of hand.

It doesn’t take the guys too long to get breakfast together since it’s only pancakes and scrambled eggs. I hadn’t realized how hungry I got, devouring my food because of it. It’s nice, all of us having a meal together like this. It'll probably happen even more often now with Laith living nearby.

Once we've all eaten, I send the guys to the family room to hang out and let the girls do whatever they want. Thayer wanted to help me with the dishes, but I wanted a moment on my own—well, sort of on my own.

Lauren picks up my call with a cheery, "Hello," that echoes through the line.

I smile at the sound of her voice. It's gotten even harder to find time to check in with each other, but we try to call at least once a week to catch up if we can.

"Merry Christmas," I say, rinsing off a dish and placing it in the dishwasher.

"Merry Christmas to you," her voice is a happy sing-song. "How's your morning been?"

"Good. The girls were up early, so I already feel like I need a nap."

She laughs. "Tell me about it. Hudson woke up every hour last night, and I wish I were exaggerating." Lauren had her first baby, a boy, in September. "I swear he's going through some sort of sleep regression, or maybe he's teething," she muses. "This mom shit is hard."

"You know you can always call me to rant."

"Even in the middle of the night?"

"Well ... " I hesitate, taking her off speaker and tucking the phone between my ear and shoulder. "Pretty soon I might be up in the middle of the night with you."

Granted, by the time my baby comes hers will be around a year old and hopefully not nearly as fussy at night.

"Why would you be—OH MY GOD." I almost drop my phone from how loud she shrieks into my ear. "You're pregnant?"

"Calm down." I stifle a laugh at her excitement, she's still squealing on the other end. "And yes, it's early still. I was going to wait to tell you, but I couldn't."

Keeping secrets from my best friend is damn near impossible.

She gasps in offense. "You weren't going to tell me?"

"I was going to tell you; I was just going to wait. That's all."

"I'm so happy for you, Salem. Are you happy?"

"Thrilled." The moment I hear my voice I know I'm sporting a dreamy, happy sort of smile.

"Hopefully we can see each other this summer. I think a trip is due. To see you guys, and my family. I miss it there."

"You do?"

"Not enough to move back," she cackles. "I'm meant for cities. I love the ... the vibrancy and constant flow too much to leave, but yeah, I do miss home at times."

"We always have room for you here." Although, I know her parents would be beside themselves if her family didn't stay with them. I like to extend the offer anyway, so she always knows she has a place with me.

"Thanks. I'll have to figure out a plan and let you know. Like I said, with work I don't think we could take a vacation until summer. Maybe not even then." She gives an annoyed huff of a sigh. "This adulting thing is great." In the background Hudson begins crying. "That's my cue to go. We'll talk soon," she promises.

I say my goodbyes, the line going silent.

Finishing up the dishes, I wash my hands before joining everyone else. I'm not sure who drug it out, but they're setting up for a game of CLUE.

Thayer notices my entrance. "You gonna play, Sunshine?"

"You know I'll never miss a chance to kick your butt at this game."

I settle on the floor beside Thayer, the others already set up and ready to go.

Not only do I beat Thayer, but I beat them all.

CHAPTER FIFTEEN

New Year's Eve

It hits me in the grocery store—that first wave of nausea with this pregnancy. My steps halt in the produce section, hand flying to cover my mouth.

Oh no, oh no, oh no.

I can't get sick in the grocery store. I'll surely die from the embarrassment.

Don't throw up. Whatever you do, don't throw up.

I'm already moving away from my shopping cart, knowing the bathrooms are all the way in the back right hand corner. The farthest spot possible from where I am.

My feet quicken on the old linoleum floors when the feeling only grows worse.

And then I'm sprinting through the store, desperate to make it to the restroom.

I'm not going to make it.

The thought hits me at the same time my eyes light upon an empty cardboard box, no doubt abandoned by an employee in the midst of stocking.

I lunge for that box like it's the holy grail, knees stinging against the hard floor. I don't care, though, not as I empty the contents of my stomach into the box. It's better than vomiting all over the floor itself. At least this is contained.

I heave again, heart lurching when I feel gentle fingers at

my nape gathering my hair back. It's such a sweet touch, like a mother's gentle caress. God, I miss my mom.

Finishing, I slowly turn around not at all surprised to see that it was Cynthia who came to my rescue. Thelma stands behind her at their cart, opening a box of saltines. I should've known it would be one or both of them. Sometimes I swear they follow me to the grocery store, the Nosy Nellies that they are.

Tearing open the plastic around the crackers, Thelma extends three of them my way. "I don't know about you, Cynthia," she begins to her partner, "but I'd say this one here is knocked up."

I let out a short laugh, chewing on the end of the saltine carefully to see how my stomach handles it. "What gave it away? Other than me blindly running through the store and throwing up in a box." I wrinkle my nose at said box. I'll have to figure out a way to get rid of that.

"Both," Thelma replies without a hint of amusement.

Cynthia huffs a sigh. "Go grab her some Ginger Ale. Make yourself useful."

Thelma grumbles something unintelligible but waddles off to do as her partner has asked.

"Feeling better?" Cynthia asks in a soft tone.

I give a jerky nod, taking a bite of the second cracker. "Thank you."

"Think you can get off the floor now?"

I look around, it only now clicking in my brain that I never stood up. "Oh."

Cynthia holds out a hand to help me up. Once I'm standing, she holds onto both my arms. "How do you feel now that you're up?"

"Fine. I'm fine." I finish the second cracker, brushing the

crumbs off my shirt.

Down on the other end of the aisle Thelma's voice reaches us. "I told you, boy, I'm not stealing. I'll pay for this when I checkout." The guy tries to take the open can of ginger ale from her, but she only clutches it tighter to her chest.

"Ma'am, you have to pay for the whole case, not just the one."

She turns to him, the two of them halting halfway to us. "You think I don't know that? I'm old, not stupid. But because I'm old, these little arms aren't in good enough shape to carry that whole box over here to where my cart is. I was going to go back and get it."

"But ma'am—"

"Make yourself useful and go get it then if you're so concerned. There's a sick lady down here and she needs her ginger ale." With that, she kicks it into overdrive, her tiny steps eating up the distance with surprising quickness. "People these days," she huffs, handing me the drink. "More concerned about me potentially stealing a measly can of soda than someone being sick." She clucks her tongue in annoyance. "I bet he'd shit his pants if he knew I stole a whole carton of cigarettes from this very store back in the day."

Cynthia turns surprised eyes to her. "You did what?"

Waving a dismissive hand, Thelma says to me, "Drink up, dear. You're starting to look a little green again."

I do as she says, knowing there's no such thing as ignoring an order from Thelma. The ginger ale does help to soothe my stomach.

"Where's your stuff, sweetie?" Cynthia asks, wrapping a gentle hand around my wrist. "We'll finish your shopping and drop it off at your house for you."

"You guys don't need to do that." The last thing I want is for my elderly neighbors to have to do my shopping on top of theirs.

"Nonsense." Thelma grabs ahold of their cart. "You need to get home and rest so your body can focus on growing that new baby—and might I add, it's not too late to use the name Thelma."

"Don't listen to her. There's no room in this town for two Thelmas." Cynthia pats my hand.

"I guess you have a point there," Thelma agrees with a huff.

We finally make it back to my abandoned cart, which is thankfully still there. "Are you guys sure about this?" I take my purse out of the cart, rifling through my wallet for some cash.

"We wouldn't offer if we didn't mean it, and put that money away, girl. We don't want it." Thelma is already waddling away with my cart.

Cynthia laughs, shaking her head. "She's right, keep your money. This is on us. Pay it forward one day." She gives a small shrug. "But I will take that." She points to my grocery list half-sticking out of my wallet.

"Right, here you go." I slip it out and extend it to her.

"Take the ginger ale." She nods to the can in my hand. "Go home and lay down, that's what that baby needs. Rest."

With those parting words, she follows in the direction Thelma went, calling after her that she needs the shopping list.

Sliding my purse onto my shoulder, I head outside to the parked car, shooting a text to Thayer while I go.

Me: The whole town will know I'm pregnant by the end of the day.

My phone rings in response as I'm settling into the driver's seat. I turn the car on, letting the call connect to the speakers Bluetooth before I answer.

"What do you mean the whole town is going to know? What happened? Are you okay?" He rattles out the questions in a rapid-fire succession. "Do I need to come get you? I told you I should be the one to go to the store."

"I'm fine." I rush to assure him before he loads up the girls and attempts to come after me. "I just got a teensy bit sick in the grocery store."

"Salem." My name is an exasperated exhale on his lips. "What happened? Stop beating around the bush."

Buckling myself in, I back out of the parking space and start my drive home all while telling him about the nausea that hit me out of nowhere and that Thelma and Cynthia were the ones to find me.

When I finally finish my tale of woe, his laughter fills the car. "You're right, the whole town will know today."

I have to laugh too. It's better than crying at least. "I guess it's a good thing we're telling the girls tonight anyway, and Laith too since he'll be there."

"Should we tell my parents now?"

I turn down the street to our house. "Might as well."

"You could sound more enthusiastic," he jokes.

"It's not that," I groan, parking in the driveway. "It's just ... not how I wanted things to go."

"That's life, Sunshine. It never goes how we want it too."

You've got me there. I'm in the driveway, so I'll be right in." I end the call and grab my bag, bracing myself for the cold I'll face the second I open the door.

I shuffle across the driveway, careful of any potential icy

spots. Thayer always does a good job keeping it free of snow and ice, but you never know. Better safe than sorry.

He must've been watching for me to make it to the porch steps, because the front door swings open. He leans there, Soleil on his hip.

"I can't believe Thelma and Cynthia are doing our grocery shopping right now."

"Me neither." I make it inside, shutting the door behind me. Sitting on the bench just inside the foyer, I yank off my boots and hang my winter coat up. "Thankfully, there was nothing embarrassing on the list."

"Like what?" He sets a wiggling Soleil down.

She runs over to me, arms wide with a shriek of, "Mommy!"

I scoop her up, plastering kisses all over her sweet cheeks.

Thayer types rapidly on his phone before tucking the device in his pocket. "I just told Cynthia to let me know when they get back so I can grab our stuff. I don't want them trying to unload our stuff and theirs."

"Where's Seda?" I look around, surprised she hasn't appeared by now.

Thayer sighs, heading for the kitchen. I follow with Soleil in my arms. "My brother and her left just a few minutes before I got your text. They're going shopping." He adds air quotes around "shopping."

"Oh? And what are they shopping for?"

He sits down at the table, a new puzzle in mid-progress. "Beats me. They didn't say, but Seda was giggling a lot, so I have a feeling whatever it is will probably make a big mess and Laith won't clean it up."

I wrinkle my nose. "Glitter's going to be involved, isn't there?"

Thayer half-smiles. "Most definitely."

***

It's only eight-o-clock, so there's no way Soleil will make it much longer. I didn't come up with some extravagant way to tell the girls. I think my brain was all tapped out after searching high and low for a way to tell Thayer. But I did order some cute shirts to gift them as way to tell them the news. Simple, sure, but better than nothing.

"Before Sol goes to bed, I have a present for you guys," I tell the girls.

Seda bounces around, her adrenaline at a high since she's convinced she'll be able to make it to midnight this year. She's been allowed to stay up on New Year's Eve the past few years, but she's always fallen asleep around ten. We'll see if this is the year she actually makes it.

"Ooh a present!" Seda hops over to me.

Soleil slowly picks her head up from Thayer's chest. "Pressie?"

"Let me grab them." I hold up a finger for them to wait.

I don't know why I feel so nervous. I know Seda will be excited, and Soleil is still at an age where she understands, but not fully.

Laith watches me from the chair with a curious expression. Binx snoozes peacefully in his lap, lightly snoring.

I grab the wrapped boxes from where I stashed them in the hall closet on the shelf. I have to stretch up on my tiptoes to get them. Letting out a breath, I close the closet behind me.

Seda jumps back and forth, frosting from a cookie dough cupcake dried on her lips. "Gimme!"

"Seda." Thayer says in as much of a scolding tone as he's capable of mustering. God knows I'm always the bad-cop parent in this house. "Sit down and wait for your mom to give it to you."

She plops her butt on the end of the couch, legs still bouncing up and down. Soleil slides off Thayer's chest, toddling over to join her sister.

"Where's my gift?" Laith jokes form his spot in the chair.

Thayer huffs a laugh. "Your gift is free rent."

Laith picks up his bottle of beer, tipping it in his brother's direction. "Fair enough."

"Can we open now?" Seda asks, trying and failing to keep the impatience out of her voice.

I bite my lip to hide my smile. "Go for it." She rips into the paper, tearing and clawing, groaning when she reaches the plain white box beneath. "Just wait a second," I tell her, helping Soleil get all the wrapping paper off. When both girls have just the box in their lap, I let Seda resume while I take the lid off Sol's box.

Seda takes the shirt out, examining the soft gray fabric. "It's a shirt."

"Turn it around," I tell her with a laugh.

She does while I unfold Soleil's shirt.

"Big Sister ... " She reads slowly, carefully, wanting to get it right. "Again." Her lips turn down. "Mommy, I think you got me the wrong shirt. It says Big Sister Again." This time, when she says it, I can see the lightbulb turn on above her head. "Wait! Are you having a baby?"

I nod, kissing her cheek, then Soleil's. "Mommy and Daddy are going to have another baby."

Seda squeals, hopping up on the couch she jumps up and

down. Soleil looks at me with wide, big eyes. "Baby?"

"Yes," I point to my belly, "there's a baby in there."

"Baby! I wuv babies." She slides off the couch, running away from me to grab her doll off the floor. She cradles it lovingly in her arms. Tears spring to my eyes. I can't wait to see her and Seda with a new baby. I know they're both going to be so good with him or her in different ways.

Seda settles back down on the couch, out of breath from all her jumping. "Do you know if it's a boy or girl?"

"No, not yet, but we'll find out when we can. It's still too early."

"Ahh!" She jumps up and down. "I'm so excited!" Wrapping her arms around my middle, she hugs me tight, then runs over to hug her dad.

"Do you have any guesses?" I ask her, gathering up the remnants of the wrapping paper from the floor. "On whether it's a boy or a girl?"

"Boy." She doesn't even hesitate in her response. "It's definitely a boy."

I press my lips together in an attempt to hide my smile. "Do you really think that or are you just hoping?"

"I know," she says with confidence, head held high. Off to my right, Soleil is still rocking her baby doll. "Forrest told me."

I don't think any of us were expecting those words to come out of her mouth. Silence descends upon the room, her shoulders curling slightly together as if she feels like she said something she shouldn't.

Laith's beer bottle clanks against the coaster when he sits down on the table behind me. I glance over my shoulder at him, his eyes steady upon his brother.

Even all these years later we've never really talked about

that time when Thayer and I were apart—when Thayer was spiraling with alcohol and in the worst place a person can be. Laith was the one who helped him through it. But I see it in his eyes, the shadows of that time—the effect that still lingers.

Thayer's eyes go glossy, gaze far away from us.

"How did he ... what do you mean he told you?" I ask her, the first to break the silence.

She swallows thickly, looking worriedly at her dad. She reaches for his hand, holding it gently in her much smaller one. He gives her a weak smile, slowly coming back to us.

"It was ... in a dream. A while ago on Halloween night. I remember because I put candy on my dresser and told him I got it for him. One of each since I don't know what he liked." I had no idea she even did that. I can tell from the surprise on Thayer's face he didn't know either. "And when I dreamed, he came to say hi. He does that sometimes." She shrugs like it's so normal for her. "He told me we were going to get a little brother, but not to say anything, so I didn't. He ... he also told me when it happened to tell Dad that it's okay and he loves him a lot and that ... " Her nose crinkles, trying to remember the conversation from the dream. "That he didn't mean it, what he said before he died."

A muscle in Thayer's jaw ticks, fighting to hold back his emotions. He fails, though, and my heart breaks when the sobs shake his body. He wraps Seda into his arms, holding on tight. He whispers something to her, and she gives a small smile, hugging him back.

I glance at Laith again, finding that he's shedding a few tears of his own, as am I.

It's always haunted Thayer, those last moments he saw Forrest alive.

I hate you. You're the worst dad ever.

It's like a weight that's been on his shoulders for far too long is finally lifted.

Thayer clears his throat. "If ... uh ... if you see him again, can you tell him I love him very much and I miss him every day." His voice cracks.

Seda nods with a small smile. "I will, but he already knows."

"Ugh," Laith groans from behind me, "no one warned me I'd be crying tonight. I need another beer." He sets Binx off his lap, heading for the kitchen.

"I'll put this one to bed," I tell Thayer, tossing a thumb at a sleepy-eyed Soleil. I want to give him time with Seda after that heavy conversation.

He nods his head in thanks.

Soleil whines a bit as I carry her up to bed, but she's tired enough that she quickly settles down once she's in bed. I read her a book, her eyes growing heavier with each word. By the time I've finished, she's out. I turn the light off, slowly sneaking my way out of her room.

I stop off in my room, tugging on a sweatshirt before rejoining the others downstairs.

I find them in the kitchen now, Laith handing Seda a glass with sparkling cider.

"Is Daddy coming over?" she asks, taking a sip of the cider. She frowns at the taste. "That's gross." She slides the glass back onto the counter.

"Um ... actually he's on a date."

Her eyes widen with excitement. "A date? Does Daddy have a girlfriend?"

"No." Her face falls at that response. "Not yet at least, but that's why people go on dates. To see if they like each other."

"I hope they like each other. Do you know who she is?"

Yes. "I'm not sure," I say instead. I want Caleb to be the one to tell her if things work out with Ms. Bloom. It's not my place to say anything to Seda yet.

She frowns. "Why didn't he tell me?"

I brush her blond hair off her forehead. "I'm sure he plans on telling you."

Rubbing her lips together, she says, "I guess."

Thayer grabs a bowl of chips and another of popcorn. "We've got a countdown to watch, guys."

"Dad," Seda sighs, clearly exasperated from the way she rolls her eyes, "we still have hours to go."

He chuckles, amused. "So, I guess that means you don't want to see your mom freak out when her favorite band plays on the TV?"

I shrill shriek leaves me. "Willow Creek is going to be on the show?"

"Yeah, based on the hints, they're the surprise guests." Laith is the one to answer me, despite the fact that he's in the middle of scarfing down a cupcake.

Running out of the kitchen, I park my butt on the couch to sit and wait for my favorite band to play. Thayer joins me, sharing a conspiratorial smile with me. I'll never forget him taking me to the concert, everything he did for me when I forgot the tickets and all the merchandise he got for me that I still love to wear. That night changed things for us. It's when my darkest secret was revealed to him.

Neither of us had any idea the journey that was in store for us beyond that night.

Willow Creek is revealed to be the surprise performer, and Seda joins me in dancing around the family room while they play their short set.

And when midnight strikes, Seda by some miracle is still awake, so we hit the poppers she picked up with Laith today, gold and silver confetti showering us and the family room. Thayer presses a kiss to one side of her cheek, my lips smashing against her other cheek. Laith watches us, laughing, but I see it in his eyes—the want for something like this.

It's coming, I want to tell him. Just like Caleb, he'll find it—his person—one day.

Before the clock can strike 12:01 Thayer pulls me into his arms. My lips part beneath his, my arms linking around his neck.

"Happy New Year, Sunshine."

I smile at him. My partner, husband, father of my children, *love of my life*.

"Happy New Year."

He kisses me again, and I have no doubt that this is about to be our best year yet.

CHAPTER SIXTEEN

The Birth

It's a strange feeling, knowing you're about to bring your last baby into the world. But I know with this baby, our family is complete. It feels right.

Thayer rubs my back, holding my hand with his other. He says nothing at how hard I squeeze his hand. Not one single complaint has been uttered from his lips since we got to the hospital a little over an hour ago. This labor is moving fast—so fast that, when I got here, they said I was past the point of an epidural.

"Do you need anything? Ice?"

I shake my head. It's all I can do at this point. With the pain, I just don't have it in me to use words. Leaning my forehead against his, I take as much support as I can from him. It feels like my body is about to split in half. It's a pain like no other, but I keep reminding myself that on the other side of this I'll get to hold my baby.

My *son*.

Seda was right.

Or, should I say, Forrest was right.

"You're doing great." Thayer tries to brush my sweaty hair away from my cheeks and forehead, but I growl—I don't know how else to describe the sound that leaves me—until he resumes rubbing my back. "You're so amazing."

"Stop talking," I beg, closing my eyes.

The pain is so intense that just hearing his voice is grating on my last nerve. I love him, but if he doesn't shut up, he's definitely going to test the limits of that love.

He gets silent after that.

Thank God.

I don't want to try to give birth handcuffed because I murdered my husband.

The door to my room opens, and the nurse comes in. "I'm going to need you to lay back so I can check you." She grabs gloves, tugging them on.

I whimper because the last thing I want to do is be on my back right now. It had to be a man that decided women should give birth on their back, legs in the air, because it's awful.

Thayer eases out from behind me. I glare at him like he's some sort of traitor. He raises his hands innocently.

The nurse checks me. "All right, Mama, it's time to push. I'm going to let the doctor know, and we're going to get things ready to rock n' roll for this little boy to make his appearance."

My eyes find Thayer's.

We're about to meet our little boy.

He grabs my hand, kissing my knuckles.

Things move in a flurry as our nurses adjust the bed for the squatting bar I requested—if I have to give birth drug free, then I'm going to do it the way I want.

Before I know it, the doctor is there and it's time to get ready to push.

Holding onto the bar, Thayer's right by my side rubbing my back in slow, soothing circles.

I don't feel nearly as tired as I did with my first two deliveries, all thanks to how fast this little boy has decided to come.

I push and I breathe, and I push some more.

I feel everything, but that fact doesn't bother me quite as much as I expected.

"Almost there," someone says. My eyes are squished closed, and I'm so concentrated on my breaths and pushing—not wanting to tear—that I'm not even sure who speaks.

A scream rips out of me and then ...

A cry.

But not mine.

A baby's cry.

My baby's cry.

My *son*.

Our son.

I sob uncontrollably, reaching for him but the doctor is extracting stuff from his nose. The wait feels like hours, not the seconds that it is while she checks his airways.

And then, he's in my arms.

He's crying. I'm crying. Thayer's crying.

So many emotions.

He's here.

"He's so beautiful." Thayer rubs his thumb over the baby's tiny head. "His hair is dark like mine, like—"

"Like Forrest's," I smile.

Our son is not a replacement for Forrest. In no way is that ever possible, but I can see how happy it makes Thayer to see that dark hair he wasn't able to pass on to our girls, is now on our son.

"He has your nose." He kisses my nose as if to emphasize his point. "And my ears."

"He's perfect."

Thayer kisses my tears away and we soak in this moment, these first moments we'll never forget with our baby. It's always a special time, a memory that I'll never forget with any of my kids.

"Hi, Samson," Thayer whispers, laying his hand over mine on the baby's back. "I'm your daddy."

Samson.

I wasn't sure I wanted to do another 'S' name. It felt a bit ridiculous, but Thayer had said at this point we should at least see if there were any we liked.

Samson—translated to sun or 'like the sun' in Hebrew.

Nothing could've been more perfect for our little boy. There's no such thing as too much sunshine. He's the answer to my hopes and dreams, the baby I worried I wouldn't get—the sunshine on a cloudy day.

Our children are the wildflowers we planted, who've grown and flourished and thrived, because of us—because we never, ever gave up.

EPILOGUE

Thirty Years Later

I'm convinced that there's nothing quite better in this world than growing old beside the one you love most. It's a privilege, unlike any other, because no day is a guarantee. I lay my head on Thayer's shoulder, our hands clasped together.

The front porch swing sways with us.

Back and forth.

Back and forth.

Flowers bloom in the yard, magnificent and thriving in the late spring weather. Thayer works religiously on the yard, and still keeps my peonies growing in the greenhouse. He might've retired years ago, but that didn't mean his love of working with the earth disappeared.

Behind the house, the wildflowers overflow the land beyond. Even to this day, it has never been developed. I'm more than a little bit grateful for that. It would've hurt to see that lovely field of flowers wiped away.

"We're lucky, aren't we? Despite it all."

I smile a little at that. "I'd say so." Luck comes in all different shapes and forms. For someone it might be getting a free coffee, for us it's just being happy. Sure, there have been moments of stress over the years—fights, pain, sadness, grieving. You name it and we've gone through it, but through it all, there's been an undercurrent of happiness. Not everyone can say that. Too often it becomes easy to dwell in the bad things, to think that's all there is to life.

"The kids should be here any minute."

Kids.

Our youngest is thirty and all of them are still kids to us.

"I know." I smile at him, using my leg to keep us swinging lightly. "Why do you think I drug you out here?"

He chuckles, eyes crinkled with age. But I love every line on his face. It's a story. A road map of our life. "Are you going to scream when you see them?"

"Possibly."

There's no point in lying. It's been too long since we had all the kids and grandkids in one place. By some miracle, they managed to all find a week that works for them. One whole week with my children and grandbabies. I don't know quite what to do with myself.

A bee flits by us, landing on a bush before taking off again.

Over the next twenty minutes, everyone arrives, and the house is once more filled with voices and the chaos of little feet running around.

It's perfect in a way I can't ever put into words.

Thayer groans, picking up one of the littlest grandsons and tickling his belly.

Looking at me with a smile, he says, "We did it, Sunshine."

I smile back.

Yeah, we did.

ACKNOWLEDGMENTS

Revisiting Thayer and Salem was an incredibly bittersweet feeling. Now, it's goodbye for real this time. There aren't the words to convey what it means to me that so many of you love them as much as I do. Writing this felt like hanging out with old friends again. It was truly a blast and I enjoyed every second of it and can only hope you felt the same reading it.

Emily Wittig, as always thank you for the amazing cover. You nail it every time. Your talent knows no bounds. But more than that, thank you for being the best friend I could ever ask for. I can't believe we've been friends for over ten years now. (Wow, look at us getting old ... okay, it's just me that's getting old.) You've been here since literally the very beginning and growing in both our lives and careers has been one of the best experiences of my life. You're one of my biggest cheerleaders and I couldn't do this without you.

Stephanie Phillips, you're so much more than my agent, you're my friend. You've been on this crazy journey since the beginning too and look where we are now. You've always believed in me (even more than I did) and I thank you for that.

Meredith Wild and the amazing team at Page & Vine—wow, thank you so much for loving and believing in these books and characters. It truly means the world to me and seeing these in stores is a dream come true. (Seriously, teenage Micalea is jumping up and down with excitement). It means everything to have a team behind these books that loves them as much as I do. That's rare and I cherish it wholeheartedly.

And finally, to you, dear reader. Thank you for reading, for the messages, likes, and tags. I couldn't do this without you guys and I never take that for granted. I love you guys so much.

ABOUT THE AUTHOR

Micalea Smeltzer is an author from Northern Virginia. Her two dogs, Ollie and Remy, are her constant companions. As a kidney transplant recipient she's dedicated to raising awareness around the effects of kidney disease, dialysis, and transplant as well as educating people on living donation. When she's not writing you can catch her with her nose buried in a book.